The Daylight Gate

Jeanette
Winterson

The
Daylight
Gate

Grove Press
New York

First published in Great Britain in 2012 by Arrow Books
in association with Hammer

Printed in the United States of America

ISBN: 978-0-8021-2163-9

Grove Press
an imprint of Grove/Atlantic, Inc.
154 West 14th Street
New York, NY 10011

Distributed by Publishers Group West

www.groveatlantic.com

13 14 15 16   10 9 8 7 6 5 4 3 2 1

To Henri Llewlyn Davies
1954–2011.
Her own witch and mine.

Introduction

The Trial of the Lancashire Witches, 1612, is the most famous of the English witch trials. The suspects were taken to Lancaster Castle in April 1612 and executed following the August Assizes.

The Well Dungeon can be visited and Lancaster Castle is open to visitors.

It was the first witch trial to be documented. Thomas Potts, lawyer, wrote his account: *The Wonderfull Discoverie of Witches in the Countie of Lancashire.* It is supposedly an eyewitness verbatim account, though heavily dosed with Potts' own views on the matter. Potts was loyal to James I – the fervent Protestant King whose book, *Daemonology*, set the tone and the feel of a century obsessed with witchcraft, and heresy of every kind — including those loyal to the old Catholic faith.

Witchery popery popery witchery, as Potts puts it, is how the seventeenth-century English understood matters treasonable and diabolical.

All of the conspirators of the 1605 Gunpowder Plot fled to Lancashire. And Lancashire remained a stronghold of the Catholic faith throughout the seventeenth century.

The story I have told follows the historical account of the witch trials and the religious background — but with necessary speculations and inventions. We do not know if Shakespeare was a tutor at Hogton Hall, but there is evidence to suggest that he might have been. The chronology of his plays, as used here, is correct. His own use of the religious, the supernatural and the macabre, is also correct.

The places are real places — Read Hall, the Rough Lee, Malkin Tower, Newchurch in Pendle, Whalley Abbey. The characters are real people, though I have taken liberties with their motives and their means. My Alice Nutter is not the Alice

Nutter of history – though why that gentlewoman was tried for witchcraft along with the Demdike and Chattox riff-raff remains a mystery.

The story of Alice Nutter and Elizabeth Southern is an invention of my own and has no basis in fact. It pleases me though, that there might have been a connection with Dr John Dee, and with Manchester, London, as well as Shakespeare himself.

And Pendle Hill is still the enigma it ever was, though the Malkin Tower is long gone.

Jeanette Winterson
June 2012

Pendle

The North is the dark place.

It is not safe to be buried on the north side of the church and the North Door is the way of the Dead.

The north of England is untamed. It can be subdued but it cannot be tamed. Lancashire is the wild part of the untamed.

The Forest of Pendle used to be a hunting ground, but some say that the hill is the hunter – alive in its black-and-green coat cropped like an animal pelt.

The hill itself is low and massy, flat-topped, brooding, disappeared in mists, treacherous with bogs, run through with fast-flowing streams plunging into waterfalls crashing down into unknown pools. Underfoot is the black rock that is the spine of this place.

Sheep graze. Hares stand like question marks.

There are no landmarks for the traveller. Too early or too late the mist closes in. Only a fool or one who has dark business should cross Pendle at night.

Stand on the flat top of Pendle Hill and you can see everything of the county of Lancashire, and some say you can see other things too. This is a haunted place. The living and the dead come together on the hill.

You cannot walk here and feel you are alone.

Those who are born here are branded by Pendle. They share a common mark. There is still a tradition, or a superstition, that a girl-child born in Pendle Forest should be twice baptised; once in church and once in a black pool at the foot of the hill. The hill will know her then. She will be its trophy and its sacrifice. She must make her peace with her birthright, whatever that means.

John Law

The pedlar John Law was taking a short cut through that nick of Pendle Forest they call Boggart's Hole. The afternoon was too warm for the time of year and he was hot in his winter clothes. He had to hurry. Already the light was thinning. Soon it would be dusk; the liminal hour – the Daylight Gate. He did not want to step through the light into whatever lay beyond the light.

His pack was bulky and his feet were sore. He slipped and put out his hand to save himself, but he sank wrist to elbow to knees into a brown bubbling mud, thick under the surface of the spongy moss. He was a heavy man. As he struggled to get up he saw the witch Alizon Device standing in front of him.

She was wheedling, smiling, flouncing her skirt. She wanted pins from his pack: *Kiss me, fat pedlar.* He didn't want to kiss her. He wouldn't give her pins. He heard the first owl. He must get away.

He pushed her roughly. She fell. She grabbed his leg to steady herself. He kicked her away. She hit her head.

He ran.

She cursed him. 'FAT PEDLAR! CATCH HIM, FANCY, BITE FLESH TO BONE.'

He heard a dog snarling. He couldn't see it. Her Familiar . . . it must be. The Devil had given her a spirit in the shape of a dog she called Fancy.

He ran. Stepping out of the furze another woman blocked his path. She held a dead lamb in her arms. He knew her: Alizon's grand-dam. Old Demdike.

He ran. The women were laughing at him. Two of them? Three of them? Or was it the Devil himself stepping through the Daylight Gate?

✢

John Law, running and falling, collapsed through the door of the Dog in Newchurch in Pendle an hour later. His lips were foamy. Men loosened his clothes. He held up three fingers and said one word: *Demdike.*

Alice Nutter

Alice Nutter rode out from the Rough Lee.

She took her pony up towards the slopes of Pendle Hill where she could look back at her house in the beginning-sun.

It was a handsome house; stone-built, oak-lined, lime trees trained to make an avenue to the door. Hornbeam hedges surrounded the house itself, and opened in wide useful squares towards her stables, poultry pens, pike pond and kennels.

Here was wealth. Her wealth. And she had not been born to it nor had she inherited it. Her fortune had come through the invention of a dye; a magenta that held fast in water and that had a curious dark depth to it – like looking into a mirror made of mercury. The Queen had ordered vats of the stuff and Alice had worked for a long time in London, with her own dye-house and warehouse.

Her knowledge of plants and their dyes, her instinctive chemistry, had recommended her to the Queen's astrologer and mathematician, John Dee. Alice had worked with him in his laboratory at Mortlake, where he used the lunar calendar of thirteen months. He believed he had succeeded in making a tiny phial of the Elixir of Life. Alice did not believe it. In any case, it had not saved the Queen or John Dee. They were both dead now.

Elizabeth had left no heir. In 1603 the English Crown had passed to James the Sixth of Scotland – now James the First of England too; a Protestant, a devout man, a man who wanted no dyes or fancy stuffs. A man who had two passions: to rid his new-crowned kingdom of popery and witchcraft.

Perhaps you could not blame him. In 1589, bringing his bride home to Scotland from Denmark, a storm had nearly drowned him. It was witchcraft, he knew it, and he had the witches tried and burned at Berwick, attending the sessions himself.

In 1605, Guy Fawkes had tried to blow him up by stacking enough gunpowder under the House of Parliament to detonate half of London . . . And every conspirator a Catholic.

The Witch Plot and the Gunpowder Plot.

But every good Catholic would see a witch tortured on the rack until her shoulders dislocated their sockets and her legs broke at the ankle and hip.

And what witch would save a Jesuit from the knife that would first castrate him, and then disembowel him, still alive?

James was fortunate that his enemies were enemies.

But Alice wondered how safe was any safety that depended on hatred?

Alice whistled. A falcon flew. One circle. One swoop. The powerful bird landed square on Alice's outstretched arm. Her long leather riding gloves were not the kind a woman wore — hers were double-stitched and heavy. Hers were scarred with the landings of the bird. As he landed she fed him a dead mouse from her pocket.

Alice was riding astride. She would not do this to attend church in Whalley or to call on her neighbour, the Magistrate Roger Nowell, or to visit the sick or to go about her business in the parish. Then she rode side-saddle and wore a magenta riding habit on top of her copper mare.

She looked beautiful. She was beautiful, even though she was – how old? Nobody knew how old. Old enough to be soon dead, and if not soon dead, then as lined and wrinkled as the milk-and-water well-behaved wives of religious husbands with their hidden mistresses. And if not that, then as toothless and foul as the hags and beldames who could afford no horses but rode broomsticks . . . some said.

This was Lancashire. This was Pendle. This was witch country.

Sarah Device

'Duck her!'

The woman on the riverbank was struggling and kicking. The man behind her held her arms back, tying her hands. Her dress was open. The man standing in front of her was tall, shaven-headed, lean-faced like a rat. He was playing with her breasts with both hands.

'This one's the Demdike witch that got away.'

Constable Hargreaves tying her hands was slower to be so sure. 'If she be a witch, Tom, then it must be proved according to the Law and the Scripture.'

'The Law and the Scripture? Her grand-dam and her sister sit in Lancaster Castle for maiming by witchcraft.'

'You got no proof of witchcraft!' said the woman.

The man called Tom hit her across the mouth. 'The pedlar John Law is a friend of mine. His legs is gone, his speech is gone. The last word he spoke was Demdike.'

'John Law spoke nowt but pigshit and drink.'

The man hit her again. She spat at him.

Constable Hargreaves had finished his knotwork. He was a lumbering man and he lumbered round to the front of Sarah Device. He held up three fingers. 'John Law held up three fingers. Three woman ran after him through the forest. If the third be not you, then say who.'

'Three women never ran after John Law in his life! He is as ugly as a boiled head.'

Tom Peeper ripped her dress away from her shoulders and down to her waist. 'Ugly? Not so ugly that you didn't lie on your back and open your legs when you wanted ribbons from his pack.'

'He was as mean as he was ugly and he was as fat as he was limp. If I had laid down under him all day I would have stood up at night still a virgin.'

'Virgin? You were born with your legs open.'

'Cats fleshed as women, that's what witches are, tempting men to sin and damnation.'

Sarah Device smiled at him. 'Let me go, Tommy, Harry. I'll give you pleasure for your pains.'

The men looked at each other. Tom undid his breeches. He had an erection. 'Do you miss your broomstick? Here's one.'

'Don't look her in the eye, Tom. She's got the Demdike eye,' said Hargreaves.

'Strip her,' said Tom. 'Search for the witch marks. A cat comes and sucks you, doesn't he, Sarah? Tibbs, is it? Or Merlin? I've seen that black cat with eyes like red coals.'

'You'll not touch me till you untie me,' said Sarah. 'And then I'll do what you want.'

'I'll do what I want now,' said Tom. 'Not when a trollop tells me I can. Stop her from wriggling, Harry.'

Tom Peeper raped Sarah Device.

He was quick. He was in practice. 'Wet as a marsh in there for you now, Harry. They're all dry, the Demdike women.'

A boy with a fishing rod was coming along the bank. He stopped and stared at the woman with her torn dress around her feet. He was about to run away but Tom Peeper went and grabbed him.

'Youth has sharp eyes. Look over her for the witch marks — go on, Robert, run your hands across her. Do you like her breasts? She can't hurt you.' He took the boy's hand and held it on Sarah's breast.

'Touch me again and I'll curse you for it.'

Tom Peeper laughed. 'You don't have the power now that Old Demdike is in the gaol. Don't be afraid of her, boy. Here . . .'

He went behind and shoved Sarah onto her knees, standing astride over her and pushing his weight onto her shoulders. She could feels his balls on her neck.

'Get your cock out, boy — she'll suck it if she wants to get home alive.'

'Let him kiss me first. I am a woman.'

Tom nodded at Hargreaves who prodded the boy to kneel down in front of Sarah. He wouldn't look at her. She leaned forward and kissed him. He tasted of fear. Sarah stopped struggling. She closed her eyes. She felt his tongue in her mouth. She was dizzy. She hadn't eaten for two days. She could feel the sun on her face and a cold shadow at her back. She could hear the sound of hooves. The Dark Gentleman would come for her soon enough. Hadn't Demdike always said so? Today, tomorrow, the next day.

The boy put his hands on her breasts, feeling the nipples. He was getting excited. She could hear voices like she was underwater. They would duck her after this. They would kill her. Today, tomorrow, the next day.

She bit.

The boy pulled back screaming low in his throat. He fainted. Sarah, with her mouth full, spat the bloody tongue onto the ground. She stood up, her mouth open, covered in blood. She started to laugh – wild hysterical laughter.

Tom unsheathed his knife from his belt. 'I'll cut your witching throat, you cat.' His hand pulled Sarah's neck back by the hair so that her throat was bare and skyward. She opened her eyes. Let him come.

The sound of a horse . . . faster now, nearer. Let him come.

Alice Nutter rode straight into Tom Peeper, knocking him down. Sarah Device got to her feet and leaned against the rump of the pony. She was shaking.

Constable Hargreaves started to mumble something about proving a witch. Alice Nutter cut him short. 'The Magistrate decides what woman will be proved. Not the mob.'

'She bewitched John Law!' said Hargreaves.

'That's a lie,' said Sarah. 'I am not accused.'

Tom Peeper got up and dragged the maimed boy up with him. He pulled Robert's hands away from his bloodied mouth. 'You see this? What woman that is no witch-woman would do this to a man?'

'What man that is a man would do this to a woman?'

The men did not reply.

'Take the boy to the herbalist in Whalley and set the charge to my account.'

'The herbalist is a witch!' said Tom.

'Yes and every midwife with her according to the likes of you. Get him away and see to him before he chokes to death on his own blood. Sarah Device – pull up your dress. You will come with me.' She passed Sarah a cloth from her saddlebag to wipe her mouth. Sarah did not speak. She could not stop shaking.

'Constable Hargreaves! Untie her.'

Hargreaves cut the cords with a single slash of his knife, not caring that he took the skin off Sarah's wrist. Then he bent down and picked up the torn-out tongue. 'Does she want this to take with her to her grand-dam Demdike in Lancaster Castle?'

Alice Nutter did not flinch. 'Wrap it and give it to me.' She stared steadily at Hargreaves until he looked away, took out his handkerchief, wrapped the object and handed it to Alice, who put it in her saddlebag.

Hargreaves looked as if he might say something but Alice Nutter was not that kind of woman.

Without glancing at Sarah, who was holding onto her stirrup leather, Alice rode off.

Hargreaves and Tom Peeper watched her go. Neither spoke until she was out of earshot. Then Hargreaves said, 'She rides astride like a man, and she rides with the bird even though no woman is a falconer. I tell you I don't trust her. A woman astride and a falcon following – that's unnatural.'

'And she took the witch's part.'

'I tell you they are the same.'

'You wouldn't be calling Alice Nutter a witch, would you, Harry?'

'I wouldn't call her nowt, Tom, leastways not in public, but there's many in private have things to say about her wealth and her power, and who she favours and who she don't – and why. Why does she let the Demdike live in Malkin Tower on her land?'

'You can't take her on.'

'Not me. There's one who would do it if he had evidence to do it.'

Tom Peeper nodded his head. 'You'd best get up to Read Hall then, Harry, and tell Magistrate Nowell what's happened.

Roger Nowell

Roger Nowell was a handsome man. He could read as well as he could ride. He liked a play as much as a cockfight. He was the Magistrate of Pendle Forest and the Master of Read Hall – the finest house in Pendle.

Old Demdike and her granddaughter Alizon had been dragged before him accused of maiming the pedlar John Law by witchcraft. Evidence against them was given by Mother Chattox. She had seen them that day at Boggart's Hole.

But Old Demdike was wily, and she had turned and faced her accuser Chattox and accused her in turn of being a witch from the womb. *Baptised twice – once for God and once for Satan. She bears the marks.*

Since they were all shouting witchcraft at each other, and since John Law was on his deathbed, Roger Nowell had a choice: pack them off to Lancaster to await trail or hand them over to the mob for a ducking that would certainly have meant a drowning.

He was hoping to quieten things down by committing them to trial – he disliked the slavering excitement of the mob. But the sensational news of this nest of witches spread long past Lancashire and soon reached London. Roger Nowell was obliged to receive an unwelcome visitor at Read Hall: Thomas Potts of Chancery Lane – Recording Clerk for the Prosecution and the Crown.

'What more do you want?' asked Roger Nowell. 'The Demdike and Chattox will be tried at the August Assizes. There is nothing more to say or to do and I would prefer to return to my regular duties when Easter is past.'

Potts fluffed himself up inside his ruff. He was a proud little cockerel of a man; all feathers and no fight. 'King James is an authority on witchcraft.

What other monarch has written his own book on the subject?'

'Your point?' said Roger Nowell.

'My point, sir, is that if you had taken the trouble to read *Daemonology* you would understand what the King in his wisdom understands; that where there is one witch there are many. Here we have four witches —'

'All in prison.'

'The Demdike has family. Mother Chattox has family. Serpents, sir. I say it again — serpents.'

Potts preferred to say things again. And again and again. Roger Nowell controlled himself.

'I have read King James's *Daemonology* and much else besides on the subject of sorcery. My mother's family was once afflicted by Demon Possession.'

'So I had heard,' said Potts.

'So I say to you as Magistrate of the District of Pendle that four witches will stand trial. None else is accused.'

Potts stalked about the room. 'Accused, no. At their filthy labours? Indeed! In all England no county is as known for its witches as Lancashire.

The abbey at Whalley, before it was destroyed by King Henry the Eighth in his just and wise Reformation, had been the sacrilegious altar of the anchorite Isolde de Heton. Anchorite become sorceress.'

'You have been studying our local history in your free time,' said Roger Nowell.

Potts had no sense of irony. 'And that lady Isolde – better call her a cat or a beldame than a lady – when she was discovered, she fled the abbey and made her fortress at Malkin Tower – now home to the witch Demdike.'

'It has been a home to sheep and pigs in the years in between. The Demdike are remote from the villages out there and make less mischief than elsewhere. The land is owned by Alice Nutter. She is a widow. She may do as she pleases with her property.'

Potts regarded him with fury. He liked to be taken seriously. 'It has been noted, sir, and by the highest in the realm, how slack you are in Lancashire to seek out and stamp out evil. Tomorrow is Good Friday. I am expecting a Sabbat on Pendle Hill.'

'Are you?' said Roger Nowell. 'I shall be in church. At Whalley.'

He was pleased to see his visitor turn purple with indignation, but Potts was not giving up.

'Since you take the evil of witchcraft so lightly, what have you to say on the other matter?'

Roger Nowell knew what was coming next.

Potts fluffed himself up again. 'Have you forgotten that only six years ago, after the Gunpowder Plot that was set to claim the life of the lawful and crowned and God-anointed King, every conspirator to a man fled to Lancashire?'

Roger Nowell had not forgotten.

'What is worse, sir? A High Mass or a Black Mass? To practise witchcraft or to practise the old religion? Both are high treason against the Crown. Witchery popery popery witchery. What is the difference?'

'Are you saying that a Mass celebrated in the name of God is a profanity? Equal to the Black Mass of the Prince of Darkness?'

'They are both diabolical,' said Potts. 'Treasonable and diabolical. Diabolical and –'

'Treasonable,' said Roger Nowell.

'I am glad we are agreed on that at least,' said Potts. 'For while so little has been done to wipe the stain of witchcraft from these lands, less has been done to prosecute those who are loyal to the King in name only and yet follow the old religion.'

'If you mean Sir John Southworth . . .'

'I do,' said Potts.

'He pays his fines as a Catholic recusant for not attending Anglican Communion and he does no harm. He is not a Jesuit. He is an old man who follows his conscience quietly. He celebrates no Mass and he hides no priests. Besides, he is my friend.'

Potts looked up at his host beadily. 'You do not choose your friends with care, sir.'

'I have known him all my life,' said Roger Nowell.

'And his son, Christopher Southworth? The Jesuit?'

Roger Nowell was uncomfortable. This was difficult.

'Christopher Southworth is a traitor – granted. If he were here I would arrest him – friendship with his father notwithstanding. But he escaped from prison after his part in the Gunpowder Plot. He is in France. You know that.'

'I know he is training priests under Father Gerard at Douai and sending them in secret to England. The English Mission is paid for and protected by the Pope himself.'

'I had heard as much. Then catch him in France.'

'We have tried. In a Catholic country we are hardly likely to succeed.'

'Then give up,' said Roger Nowell.

Potts's small eyes widened. 'Give up? The reward is vast. And think of the glory. The advancement. If I were instrumental in the capture of Christopher Southworth, King James would raise me up.'

Roger Nowell would gladly have raised Potts up and thrown him on the fire. Instead he forced himself to speak reasonably.

'Christopher Southworth is a traitor but not a fool. If he set foot in Lancashire I would know it within a day. He will never return here.'

'He might,' said Potts. 'I have had his sister arrested.'

Roger Nowell was taken aback. 'Jane? She is Protestant! She is the one Southworth who has renounced the old religion – Sir John won't speak to her – you can hardly arrest her for –'

'For witchcraft,' said Potts.

'But that is foolery!'

'You take it all too lightly it seems to me. She has been accused of causing mortal sickness by sticking pins into a poppet. Her maid fell ill like to die. The maid's mother found the poppet pinned and bristling like a hedgehog. Jane Southworth has been arrested.'

'House arrest?'

'She is in Lancaster Castle.'

'With the Demdike and Chattox?'

Before Roger Nowell could press Potts more on this, Harry Hargreaves was shown in.

Constable Hargreaves began to explain in his slow lumbering way about Sarah Device and Alice Nutter. Roger Nowell could barely contain his irritation. He wasn't listening. He didn't like Alice

Nutter but he was hardly going to accuse her of witchcraft. He was far more concerned about Potts and the Southworths.

Potts was delighted by Hargreaves's news. He was all for them riding out to Malkin Tower right away, but Hargreaves had some further interest to add.

'My spies have reported a band of persons travelling through the forest – unknowns – vagrants they could be, yes, begging for alms at Easter – or they could be to do with the Good Friday Black Mass that we have suspicions of tomorrow, on Pendle Hill.'

Potts rejoiced at this possibility and ordered Hargreaves to get him some men. They would go to the top of Pendle Hill and lie in wait.

Roger Nowell was relieved to see them leave together. Potts couldn't have arrived in Lancashire at a more inconvenient time. Witchcraft did not interest Roger Nowell; superstition and malice, he thought. He had spies of his own at work and he was waiting for other news.

Is that him? The Jesuit?

Yes.

Shall we take him?

Follow him.

Where will he go?

To Lancashire, where his home is. To Pendle Forest, where his heart is.

Malkin Tower:
Good Friday 1612

It was a strange, wild, ragged group of men and women beginning to arrive at Malkin Tower.

Mouldheels had walked from Colne, begging, cursing and spitting all the way, trailing her familiar stink behind her, and bringing no broomstick with her, only a cat as clean as his mistress was rotten. Mouldheels had flesh that fell off her as though it were cooked. And her feet stank of dead meat. Today they were wrapped in rags already beginning to ooze.

There was pretty Margaret Pearson from Padiham, getting food from her favours given to farmhands. The Puritan who owned the mill called her a ditch-trollop and beat her if she came round looking for barley. But his son never turned her away. Fornication was a sin but not with a witch who had put a spell on you.

John and Jane Bulcock were there; some said they were husband and wife, others said brother and sister though they slept in the same bed.

Old Demdike's disfigured daughter Elizabeth had called the meeting. Her son James, 'Jem' Device, had stolen a sheep to roast for the feast.

And there was the little girl Jennet Device, vicious, miserable, underfed and abused. Her brother took her with him to the Dog to pay for his drink. Tom Peeper liked his sexual conquests to be too young to fall pregnant.

The tower had not been so busy for a long time. The table was roughed out of a few planks set on trestles and there were no plates. The mutton spitting above the smoking fire was torn off the carcass and served straight onto the table. Each person had brought a cup to be filled with ale.

Malkin Tower was a squat stone round of a

building, soundly constructed and strangely placed, alone and remote, with no purpose anyone could remember, and no inhabitants anyone ever knew but for the family they called the Demdike.

The tower might have been a prison — it stood like one, grim and windowless, except for slits that looked east and west, north and south, like narrow suspicious eyes. There was a stagnant moat around the tower, filled with thick green algae. The sun did not shine here.

It was nearly noon, and there were eleven of them present when Alice Nutter rode up with Sarah Device walking beside her. Squint-eyed Elizabeth came out to meet them. She bowed briefly. 'Mistress Nutter!'

Alice acknowledged her but without warmth. 'Sarah was on her way to me yesterday, bringing a message from you, she says, when she fell foul of Tom Peeper and Constable Hargreaves. My advice to you and your family is to stay away from either man.'

The child Jennet came out of the tower. Bare

feet. Ragged dress. Pinched and starved, she gnawed jealously on a piece of fatty mutton, like a wilder thing than a child.

Alice Nutter dismounted her pony and took loaves, butter, apples and a large cheese from her saddlebag. She gave them to Elizabeth. 'When did that child last eat?'

'Three days ago, like the rest of us. The parson calls Lent a fast, for it suits the church to starve the poor. I begged from the church and the parson said that a fast did a woman good. I answered that I must be the goodliest woman in Pendle.'

Alice tossed Jennet her own bread and cheese. The child made off with them into the bushes.

'What is it you want from me?' asked Alice.

'Please to come inside, Mistress.'

It was a strange sight. It was a strange company.

The dinner guests were smeared in grease and fat. The rough plank table now had the remains of the sheep carcass in the centre, a hacking knife stuck into its middle. Most of the sheep had been eaten. There was a jug of ale on the floor and a pot of turnips steeping over the fire.

As Alice entered, the company stood up and bowed to her.

Elizabeth Device was behind her, with Sarah Device. 'Now we are gathered thirteen,' she said.

Alice Nutter began to realise what this was about. 'I am not one of your thirteen,' she said.

She turned to leave. Jem Device was behind her at the door. He was leaning on it, a rough axe in his hand. Alice looked around. The tower had no other door and no other means of escape. She was aware of a powerful smell of rot.

'I called this meeting,' said Elizabeth Device, 'that all of us here might free my mother Demdike and my daughter Alizon from Lancaster Castle. I will even free the Chattox if they will help us.'

Agnes Chattox nodded her head.

'What has this to do with me?' said Alice. 'If you wish me to speak with Roger Nowell on your behalf I will do so. Not because you are witches, but because you are not. Witchcraft is superstition.'

There was a murmur round the table. Elizabeth spoke again.

'Alice Nutter. My mother, Old Demdike, knew

you well, do you deny it?' Alice did not reply. Elizabeth continued. 'You were her friend once, in better times, in times forgotten. You have the gift of magick and you learned it from the Queen's own magician, John Dee.'

'John Dee is dead,' said Alice. 'He was not a magician, he was a mathematician.'

'And Edward Kelley? Was he a mathematician too?'

Alice was surprised. Edward Kelley was the most famous of the mediums and spirit-raisers. He had been an intimate of John Dee in Manchester and at Mortlake. He had been Alice Nutter's lover too. Many years ago. He was long dead.

'What do you want from me?' said Alice again.

'Blow up the gaol at Lancaster and free Old Demdike and Alizon and the Chattox and her daughter Nance Redfern. Spirit them away. It is not too much for a woman of your magick and we here will serve you as we served Old Demdike.'

'I never served Old Demdike,' shouted Agnes Chattox.

'The general point is good,' said Elizabeth. 'And

as for you, Agnes Chattox, will you or won't you serve Mistress Nutter?'

'I will if she can make a spell.'

'I cannot make a spell,' said Alice. 'I have no magick.'

'Then how did you come by your money? Then how did you come by your youth? Look at you, unlined and strong, and yet you are not so much younger than Old Demdike and she is eighty.'

The company was astonished. Alice was uneasy yet she kept calm. 'I am not the age you reckon. I knew your mother when I was young and she had her own ways of seeming youthful. It was that Demdike had youth when others had age, not that I had age and now I have youth.'

This answer was sufficiently confusing, and the company were all convinced of the powers of Old Demdike. Then Jem Device began kicking the door with his heel. 'Make her do it, make her swear!'

The rest at the table began banging the table in rhythm with Jem's kicking. 'Make her do it, make her swear, make her do it, make her swear!' The pounding and the chanting got louder and wilder. They were drunk already and now they were intoxicating themselves with the thought of power.

Jem Device came round to the table and threw down his axe. He took out a knife and held it out to his mother.

'Take her blood – make her swear.'

Elizabeth was white. 'I cannot take her, Jem. She is too powerful.'

'She is not too powerful to bleed,' shouted Jem. He came up fast on Alice with his little knife and slashed her arm. She bled.

The blood seeped through her sleeve and began to drip onto the floor. The assembled company scrambled towards it, wiping it with their hands, licking their fingers. Alice felt like she was being attacked by rats, and the more she pushed the more they crowded.

Alice was in danger and she knew she had only one chance. She took it. She shouted, 'Get on your knees!'

The company fell back, afraid. Alice repeated her command and, taking the knife from James Device, still standing, she told him to kneel before her. He did so.

Alice Nutter did not hesitate. She pulled open his shirt and scored a triangle in blood opening it out to make a shallow bleeding pentagram on his bare chest. He was trembling with terror.

'James Device, you will answer to me, your mistress, in all that you do, and if you do not, Satan will take your soul. Do you hear me?'

'Yes, Mistress.'

'Feed on him.'

She stood back as the company fell on James as they had on her. He was covered in them, like leeches, like bats. Only Elizabeth and Sarah did not do it.

'You will lead us then?' said Elizabeth.

Before Alice could answer there was a fierce banging at the door. The creatures feeding on James Device stopped their foul meal and pulled themselves up. The banging came again.

'Open this tower in the name of the Magistrate.'

Alice made a gesture with her hand for everyone to resume their places. James tied his shirt at the neck. Alice stood back. Elizabeth opened the door.

Outside stood Roger Nowell, Constable Hargreaves and Tom Peeper.

Confrontation

'Your riding coat is torn,' Roger Nowell said as he stood before Alice Nutter.

'My pony bolted,' Alice replied, meeting his gaze.

'A feast, I see,' said Roger Nowell, 'and meat too, on Good Friday, when it is the rule that fish should be eaten.'

'The poor have their own rules,' said Alice. 'The poor must eat what they can when they can. There were no alms from the church or from yourself, or from any other person, given to the Demdike this Easter. I came with provisions of my own. That is the purpose of my visit.'

'Did you bring that sheep?' asked Roger Nowell.

'James Device – I am arresting you for the theft of a sheep,' said Constable Hargreaves.

'Prove it!' shouted Elizabeth. 'The Demdike have known suffering enough from you.' She turned to Roger Nowell. 'And from you, good Magistrate of the Law. I'd like to see the pair of you in the stocks in the quick and handy way you fasten up my kind. I'd like to see you being pelted with rubbish and soaked in day-old piss.'

Hargreaves hit her across the face. She spat at him.

Roger Nowell looked at her with disgust. Elizabeth Device was dirty and ugly. The strangeness of her eye deformity made people fear her. One eye looked up and the other looked down, and both eyes were set crooked in her face. Her hair was already white, although she was not yet forty, and her skin had shrunk tight and sallow over her bones. She had been married once, but she and her children had come back to Malkin Tower to live with Old Demdike. Sometime, perhaps nine years ago, she had been raped. The ragged child Jennet Device was the result of the rape.

Elizabeth was fierce. Begging had never helped her. If she could not gain sympathy, she could provoke fear and dislike.

Roger Nowell looked around at the company – threadbare and drunk, stinking and defiant. He said, 'We have intelligence that a Sabbat is planned on Pendle Hill. You are thirteen in number. Thirteen is a witch number and the number of a coven to defy the twelve and one that was Christ and his Disciples. You profane the day by eating meat. Your kin has confessed to witchcraft. You will remain under guard at Malkin Tower for questioning and for proving – by whatever means we see fit.'

Alice Nutter stepped forward. 'And if Sarah Device was dead in the river this morning, would you charge Tom Peeper and Constable Hargreaves with murder?'

'Putting to death a witch is not murder. It is the law of the Scripture,' said Constable Hargreaves. '"Thou shalt not suffer a witch to live." Exodus Chapter 20 Verse 16.'

Roger Nowell looked at Alice Nutter. He was

puzzled. 'I am surprised to find you here, Mistress.'

'Your number of thirteen includes myself. Am I a witch? It includes that ragged child – is she a witch?' Jennet Device was darting round the door.

Alice picked up her gloves and walked down the steps from the tower.

'You letting her go?' said Tom Peeper.

Tom Peeper and Roger Nowell followed Alice out to where she was untying her pony.

'Mistress Nutter, I am the Magistrate of the District of Pendle,' said Roger Nowell, 'I must take these matters seriously. John Law is on his deathbed. Demdike and Chattox are self-accused.'

'She takes the witches' part,' said Tom Peeper. Without warning, he lunged forward and grabbed Alice's pony. Alice dashed him across the shoulders with her riding crop but his darting twisted face was triumphant. 'Search her saddlebag, go on, she knows what she's got in there, and so do I!'

Alice stepped back. Roger Nowell put his hand in one of the leather bags and came out with a handful of cobnuts. He threw them to the ground, keeping his eyes on Alice as he searched and dipped into the second bag. He drew out the handkerchief, soaked in blood.

'What in God's name is this?'

'It is Robert Preston's tongue,' said Alice Nutter.

'She took it to make a Devil's poppet!' shouted Tom Peeper.

'I took it as evidence,' said Alice. 'You threatened Sarah Device with ducking and you raped her.'

'So she says,' said Tom Peeper. 'The young lad was kissing her in sport. It was sport, Master Nowell.'

Roger Nowell held the black and swollen tongue away from him. Then he threw that body part into the bushes. He said: 'Mistress Nutter, I will ask you to attend me at Read Hall at six o'clock this evening.'

Alice nodded her head, mounted her pony, and turned to go. Then she reined in for a moment and said to Roger Nowell, 'I provided the sheep.'

Hidden in the bushes, the child Jennet Device had seen everything. As soon as the men were gone, she darted out and snatched the cobnuts and went to look for what else had been thrown nearby.

It Begins

Alice Nutter was in her study when she had the distinct feeling that she was being watched.

Her study was panelled in oak, with a large oak table under the window and two silver candlesticks on that table.

She was sitting reading a letter sent to her many years ago by her lover Edward Kelley. He had sent it soon after she and he and John Dee had been in Amsterdam together undertaking certain alchemical experiments. Edward Kelley had raised a spirit, a Familiar he called Trumps, and in his letter he promised Alice that should she ever be in difficulty, she could call on Trumps. The method of doing so was in the letter, along with a faded lock of Edward Kelley's hair.

Alice laid down the letter. She was troubled by the happenings of the day, and troubled by something that she did not yet understand. She stood up and went to the window. The air outside was mild but her study had become cold and strangely dark. She closed the window, took the tinderbox and lit her candles, watching the flames leap and burn. The room felt better now, but she was still cold, and so she bent to make a fire out of stacked applewood in the big open hearth. A servant could have done it for her, but Alice had always enjoyed lighting her own fire. The wood caught and crackled.

Soon she would have to ride over to Read Hall for her appointment with Roger Nowell.

She turned back to Edward Kelley's letter. She read aloud: '*And if thou callest him, like unto an angel of the north wearing a dark costume, he will hear thee and come to thee. Yet meet him where he may be met — at the Daylight Gate.*'

There was a rush of air through the room. The

new fire flared high and the flames pushed forward from the hearth, catching the little fire screen and igniting it.

Alice jumped up towards the burning screen, and as she did so she heard a man say her name. 'Alice Nutter . . .'

She smothered the fire screen with her bare hands, left it smouldering, and went to the study door. She opened it onto the long, dark corridor that led to her bedroom. She looked this way and that; there was no one in the corridor.

She went back inside and closed the door. She had a feeling of foreboding. Her study felt *occupied* – that was the word that jumped into her mind. *Occupied* . . . and not by a person, but by a presence.

'Who is here?' she said. There was no reply, only the intensity of the feeling. She said it again. 'Who is here?' This time there was a movement by her desk under the window. The window was fastened, so it could not be a draught.

The letter from Edward Kelley lay on the desk. As she watched, the letter was picked up – that was the only way to describe it – picked up as if someone were reading it. The letter hovered in the air, held by what? An invisible hand? An unearthly wind? The letter was too near the candle flame and whatever was holding it began to move it nearer. Alice watched as if she were hypnotised. The thick paper began to scorch. Alice roused herself, jumped forward and grabbed the letter — as she took it she knew that something was holding it there. She summoned her courage.

'I will act when I am ready,' she said. 'Now get gone.'

The window opened wide. A rush of air blew across the study. The fire had died down. The candles were steady.

Alice closed the window and took care to latch it. She folded the letter. As she did so, she saw that where the scorch mark had extended the ink the letters seemed raised up. 'The Daylight Gate.' That was what the presence wanted her to read.

She opened a small cupboard filled with phials and powders and put the letter between the bottles. She locked the cupboard. Then, as a precaution, she took a piece of chalk and drew a symbol on the back of her study door. She had never done this before but she had seen John Dee do it many times.

Was it protection? Was it warning? Was it recognition?

Already she was beginning the route she had never wanted to begin. The Left-Hand Path they called it.

She did not believe in witchcraft, but she had experience of her own that there was such a thing as magick. *Magick is a method,* John Dee had said, *no more, no less than a means of bringing supernatural forces under human control.*

She felt she was in danger. She would have to use what methods she could to save herself. It would not be the first time.

Outside her window she heard her servant trotting out her copper mare. She went to change into her magenta riding habit. It was time to keep her appointment with Roger Nowell.

Read Hall

Read Hall was a confident, handsome building, old and large, riddled with medieval rooms and extended with later additions. The Nowell family had lived there since the 1400s. Roger Nowell was proud of his house and proud of his line.

The moon lit up the courtyard well enough but Roger Nowell's serving man was waiting with a flare. As Alice Nutter rode up, a second man ran out to take her horse. She slipped easily out of the side-saddle. Her body was lithe and strong.

Roger Nowell was a widower. Alice Nutter was a widow. They were both rich. They could have been a match. Alice's land abutted Read Hall. But they had not courted; they had gone to law. Roger

Nowell claimed a parcel of land as his. Alice Nutter claimed it as hers. She had won the lawsuit. Roger Nowell had never lost anything before – except his wife.

The servant showed her into the study where the fire was piled high. A bottle and two goblets waited on a small table. It was a masculine room that smelled of tobacco, but not unpleasantly. He had books, writing paper. She liked it.

The firelight and the candlelight lit up her magenta riding habit so that it had the curious effect of seeming as though it were made of water that was on fire. The luminescence of the dye was the secret of Alice's fortune.

Roger Nowell entered and she turned to him smiling. He was taken aback for a moment; what a beautiful and proud woman she was. He smiled too.

He did not ask if she wanted wine but poured it for her into one of the silver goblets. 'Hospice de Beaune,' he said. 'A Jesuit brought it back from Burgundy.'

He drank and refilled his own goblet. 'Damn

pity about the papists. They have better wine than the Protestants.'

'And even the Protestants have better wine than the Puritans.'

Roger Nowell laughed. 'Mistress Nutter . . . do not mistake me. I do not much care what form of worship a man chooses, or whether his conscience is guided by a priest or his own prayers. I do not much care if a stupid old woman thinks Satan can feed her when others won't. But I am a practical man and I have to do my duty.'

'What is your duty tonight?'

'To question you about the Demdike.'

'Lancashire is brim-full of witches, it seems,' said Alice Nutter.

'So our visitor Master Potts believes. He is shivering on the top of Pendle Hill watching the sky for broomsticks.'

He poured her more wine. He was dressed in black velvet and he walked softly like a panther. She had never found him attractive before. He raised his goblet, smiling. 'Here's to Potts, our draughty little lawyer from London.'

They drank. He said, 'I do not like lawyers and their meddling.'

'Yet you took me to court over the land.'

It was the wrong thing to say. His mouth closed from a smile to a line. He was no longer genial. 'You know my position on that land – I still believe it is mine but I am willing to abide by the law.'

'As am I, sir. But as for the law and witchcraft, the Demdike are to be pitied, not punished.'

'The meeting at Malkin Tower was for some purpose, Mistress, and I believe you know what that purpose was. Will you tell me?'

'If they think they are witches does that make them so? They will not be escaping Malkin Tower by broomstick however much Master Potts wants to see them fly over Pendle Hill.'

Roger Nowell nodded his head, silent for a moment. 'And yet the Demdike live on your land.'

'That is charity, sir, not a lease from the Dark Gentleman.'

'You know that gentleman perhaps?'

Alice was perplexed. She had not expected this.

She turned away. He stepped round in front of her, handsome, dangerous.

'I am not accusing you of being a hedge-witch. Demdike and Chattox deal in dolls with pins stuck in them and horseshoes turned upside down to drain a man's luck and maybe his life. Did they maim John Law? I am sure he ran so fast his heart burst.'

'Then . . .' said Alice. 'I do not see . . .'

Roger Nowell held up his hand. 'I have travelled in Germany and the Low Countries. Do you know the story of Faust?'

'I saw Kit Marlowe's play *Doctor Faustus* when I lived in London.'

'Then you know that Faust makes a pact with Satan through his servant Mephistopheles. That pact brings immense wealth and power to those who will sign it in blood. Such men and women are unassailable. They triumph in lawsuits, for example.'

Roger Nowell paused. Alice felt sick. She said nothing.

'The wealth of such persons is often a mystery.

They will buy a fine house, find ample funds, and yet, where does the money come from?'

Alice rounded on him now. She was angry. 'My fortune comes from my industry. I had a royal warrant from the Queen.'

'And instruction from the magician John Dee,' said Roger Nowell. 'I know more of your past than you imagine. My mother's family, the Starkies, were possessed by demons for a time, and had to consult John Dee when he was living in Manchester.'

'I know of that,' replied Alice, 'and that John Dee succeeded where Puritan preachers failed.'

'That is exactly my point,' said Roger Nowell. 'By what means he succeeded we cannot know, but like can talk with like.'

'John Dee is dead and cannot answer your charges. Let him rest in peace.'

'If he does rest . . . He died in 1608, but some say they have seen him in Pendle – visiting you.'

The room was heavy like a great iron weight was slowly dropping from the ceiling.

'Let me read to you,' said Roger Nowell. 'It is a night for reading.'

He went to his desk and came and stood opposite her with a leather-bound book. 'This volume is titled *Discourse of the Damned Art of Witches*, and is written by a man well known to me – a Professor of Divinity at Cambridge. Please, sit down. Listen to what he has to say.

'*The ground of all witchcraft is a league or covenant made between the witch and the Devil, wherein they do mutually bind themselves the one to the other . . . the Devil . . . for his part promises to be ready to his vassal's command, to appear at any time in the likeness of any creature, to consult with him, to aid and help him.*'

Roger Nowell closed the book and looked directly at Alice. 'You have a falcon. Is that your Familiar?'

'What is it that you want from me? The land in dispute?'

Roger Nowell shook his head. 'I do not like to lose but I do not like to dwell on my losses either. That matter is done.'

'Then what is this about?'

'Explain the matter at Malkin Tower.'

'I went there at the request of Elizabeth Device.

I took nourishment with me. I agreed with Elizabeth Device that I would intercede with you on behalf of her family.'

'On behalf of self-confessed witches?'

'Such women are poor. They are ignorant. They have no power in your world, so they must get what power they can in theirs. I have sympathy for them.'

'Sympathy? Elizabeth Device prostitutes her own children.'

'And what of the men who buy? Tom Peeper rapes nine-year-old Jennet Device on a Saturday night and stands in church on Sunday morning.'

'You rarely stand in church yourself,' said Roger Nowell.

'If you cannot try me as a witch perhaps you will charge me as a papist. Is that it?'

'Your family is Catholic,' said Roger Nowell.

'And every family in England till King Henry left the Church of Rome. The Church of England is not yet a hundred years old and you wonder that many still follow the old religion?'

'I do not wonder about that,' said Roger Nowell. 'But I wonder about you.'

They were both silent for a time.

'You are stubborn,' said Roger Nowell.

'I am not tame,' said Alice Nutter.

He stood up and came over to her chair. She could smell him; male, tobacco, pine. He was so close she could see the grey beginning in his beard. He took her hand. He held it up to the light, looking at it as he spoke softly. 'You mistake me if you imagine I believe in no dark power. I believe in God and therefore I believe in the Devil.'

'Who surely has better things to do than help the Demdike dry up cattle, steal sheep and bewitch pedlars?'

'Indeed. At the Berwick witch trials many of the women were poor and ignorant, deluded by a pretence of power. Yet their leader was a man who would risk anything to kill a king. Suppose our Lancashire witches have found such a leader? Someone whose knowledge of the magick arts is directly from the Devil himself? Faust was a man who made such a pact. But a woman? Where beauty met with wealth and power. What might she not accomplish?'

'I have no special power.'

'Like Faust you have strange youthfulness. Many wonder at you, undiminished by time.'

'I am skilled in herbs and ointments.'

Roger Nowell nodded. 'Will you give evidence against the Demdike?'

'I have no evidence to give.'

He stood up, stretching. He smiled. 'Then, perhaps you will attend the trial yourself in a different capacity. That is not my wish, though it may become my duty. But for now, I should like to invite you to a play.'

Alice was utterly bewildered.

'We ride at dawn to Hoghton Tower. There is a new play to be put on, written by William Shakespeare who has had great success in London. He was a tutor for a time at Hoghton Tower and, by gracious request, his play is to be performed there.'

'I have seen some of his plays in London,' said Alice. 'What play is this?'

'*The Tempest.* I am told it is a play about magick.'

Before Alice could answer a servant ran into the

room. Roger Nowell followed him at once into the square hall. The front door was open. There were dogs barking outside.

Alice went forward. In the hall were two men she had never seen before. They were dirt-spattered and sweat-stained. One was wiping his face with a wet cloth.

'Where did you lose him?' said Roger Nowell. 'Salmsbury Hall?'

One of the men looked back towards Alice. Roger Nowell turned, gesturing with his hand as though all this were nothing of any importance. 'A fugitive. Unexpected. One of my men will ride with you to the Rough Lee as you have brought no servant.'

Alice was escorted to her horse. In the courtyard were half a dozen men carrying wild and burning flares. Stag-hounds ran about, some with their noses to the ground, others sniffing the air as though they were hunting ghosts.

As she rode the short distance to the Rough Lee she watched the flares dipping and darting between the trees as the men ran following the dogs. The dark forest looked on fire. The trees were lit up like funeral pyres. She thought she saw bodies strapped to the trees, burning, burning, burning.

She spurred her horse.

The men were moving away from the direction of her house, towards the river. The moon came up, shining down. Her horse shied. On the path directly in front of the horse's hooves stood a huge hare, all eyes, ears and startle.

The hare had a look she knew. But that was foolish. It was a hare.

She rode on, and dismissed Roger Nowell's servant at her gate.

She was already unbuttoning her riding habit as she climbed the staircase to bed. She was in her shift when she opened the door from her dressing room into her bedroom.

Christopher Southworth was lying on her bed.

Christopher Southworth

His eyes were blue like forming crystals. There was a scar across his face from his left eyebrow to his right lip.

Alice had not seen him for six years. She had never expected to see him again. There was a knock at the bedroom door. Alice threw a cover over Christopher and opened the door to take in the chicken pie and wine she had asked for. She locked the door and pulled the heavy curtains across the window.

'Is it you they are hunting, Kit?'

'Give me food first.'

They were like children; eating quickly, laughing, her heart beating too fast, his face smiling all the time as he ate. He had got into the house after dark and taken the little staircase to her study, and crept through the secret corridor that joined her bedroom. Alice ran her hand over the ridge of scars under his eyes and kissed his eyelids where the skin was thick like leather.

When he had been captured after the Gunpowder Plot his torturers had cut his face with a hot iron. They had blinded him by dripping wax into his pinned-back eyeballs. The curious blue of his eyes was due to the elixir that had saved his sight. But nothing could hide the scars.

'You should not have come back to England, Kit. They will hang you this time.'

Christopher Southworth nodded and drank more wine. 'I had to come. Jane has been arrested on charges of witchcraft.'

'Jane? Jane is a Protestant! The only member of your family to receive the Anglican Communion.'

'It is a trap, I know.'

'Do they want your head so badly?'

'They will not stop till all of the Gunpowder Plotters are dead. King James has set his sights on Lancashire, Alice. He believes that this is the county of England where he has the most to fear – from Catholic traitors or from witching hags.'

'Demdike and Chattox have been taken for trial at Lancaster Castle.'

'I know. Jane is in there with them. They are in the Well Dungeon until the August Assizes. She will not survive that ordeal – instant death would be more merciful.'

'I have just come from Roger Nowell. He said nothing to me of this.'

Alice told Christopher about the matter at the Malkin Tower. He was listening carefully, restless, tapping his fingers on the bedpost.

'None of this is coincidence or chance. There is danger here. Alice. Listen to me. Withdraw. Apologise. Equivocate. Do not risk yourself for that broken family of vagrants and thieves they call the Demdike.'

Alice drew away from him. 'Are you like all other men after all? The poor should have no justice, just as they have no food, no decent shelter, no regular livelihood? Is that how your saviour Jesus treated the poor?'

Southworth was ashamed. Only Alice Nutter talked to him like this. He was used to high theological arguments, great causes, single-minded passions, and she reminded him that every day poor people suffer for no better reason than that they are poor.

'You are right,' he said, 'but there will be no justice.'

Alice shook her head. 'All the more reason that there should be love.'

'Love? For the Demdike?'

Alice said, 'You have a god to forgive you your past. I carry mine with me every day.'

'Why do you call Him my God? Who is yours?'

Alice did not answer. She was standing up, looking out of the window into the dark and empty courtyard. She said, 'I will tell you the story of Elizabeth Southern.'

Elizabeth Southern

Her family were from Pendle Forest as mine are, but separated by the hill. We did not know each other. Her family had a reputation for witchcraft but I had no interest in that.

I was married early to Richard Nutter and when he died just as early I was left to fend for myself. That is when I went to work in Manchester, at the Cloth Fair, trading some of my dyes and stuffs.

I was at my stall one morning when a grave and distinguished gentleman came to me and asked me the date of my birth. I told him, with some surprise, and he quickly made a calculation, nodding his head all the time. Satisfied, he asked me if I would meet him at an address that night. He told me to have no fear – it was in connection with the Great Work, he said. Alchemy, he said. 'My name is Doctor John Dee.'

I went to the house at the appointed hour. There were two other people in the room besides John Dee: a man called Edward Kelley and the woman Elizabeth Southern.

This woman had been working for John Dee for over a year. She had a flair for mathematics and he had taught her how to work out the astrological computations he needed for his work. He used the lunar calendar of thirteen months.

Edward Kelley was a medium. He claimed he could summon angels and other spirits.

John Dee asked me if I would be the fourth of the group. He said he had seen it in my face and confirmed it by my nativity.

I asked him what he had seen but all he said was that I would be suitable for the Work.

He offered me a sum of money and proposed that we should pursue the Work in Manchester until such time as we would leave for London.

I had no reason to go home to Pendle and no reason to stay in Lancashire and so I agreed.

Several months later I was making a preparation of mercury when Edward Kelley came in and announced that Saturn was favourable for the double-coupling. He brought John Dee into the chamber and asked that we all make ourselves naked and invoke the higher power.

John Dee did not want to do this but Edward told him that an angel had appeared to him in a dream to say that our bodies should be shared in common. The Great Work was to dissolve all boundaries. The Great Work was to transform one substance into another – one self into another. We would merge. We would be transformed.

I was shy and modest. Elizabeth Southern was not. She asked Edward Kelley to take the long bellows and billow up the flames in the furnace and warm the room. While he was about it, she took thick sheep fleeces from the cupboard and spread them over the floor. Then she undressed.

I have never seen a more beautiful body on a man or a woman. She was slender, full, creamy, dark, rich, open, luxurious. In her clothes she was like any other well-formed woman, but naked she seemed like something other than, or more than, human. I do not say like a goddess but like an animal and a spirit combined into human form. *An angel*, Edward Kelley said.

Both men were erect. They moved to touch her and she kissed them both equally. She had no shame, no fear. What did I feel? I did not feel desire or fear. I felt proud. Does that seem odd to you? I was proud of her.

John Dee and Edward Kelley had intercourse with her in turn. When it was done John Dee went back to his books, for he was never comfortable with much that was not a book. Edward Kelley fell asleep. They had forgotten me and I had not minded.

It was evening and the room was hot now and the fire was red in the furnace and we had drunk wine. I was naked but covered.

Elizabeth leaned up on one arm smiling at me. Looking into her eyes was like looking into another life. She kissed me on the lips. She put her hand between my legs and stroked me until I had nothing in my mind but the colour of magenta.

'This is our love,' she said.

Another year passed and all four of us moved to London where John Dee had a laboratory at Mortlake. Then Edward Kelley and John Dee went for a time to Poland. For almost a year Elizabeth and I were alone.

We rented a warehouse at Bankside where we proceeded with the alchemical work, and where I discovered, quite by chance, the secrets of the dye that has been the foundation of my fortune.

That year 1582 was the happiest year of my life. Elizabeth and I were lovers and we lived as lovers, sharing one bed and one body. I worshipped her. Where I was shy, she was bold, and where I was hesitant, she was sure. I learned life from her and I learned love from her as surely as I learned astrology and mathematics from John Dee and necromancy from Edward Kelley.

One night there was a performance at the

Curtain Theatre in Shoreditch, a mean and riotous place, but a place we enjoyed. I do not remember what we saw, but the Queen herself was there.

It so happened that I had perfected my magenta dye and I had a dress made that I had dyed myself. I wore it to the performance and every head in the theatre turned to stare at me, such was the shimmer and depth of the hue.

The next day the Queen sent for me.

And that was the beginning of my fortune and the beginning of my trials.

Elizabeth was jealous. She was a jealous woman by nature, and she was jealous of my success and of my money. I was at fault because I did not share everything equally with her. As I grew wealthier I invested my money. I bought her anything she wanted but I would not make her equal.

And I was no longer interested in the Great Work. What did I care about turning lead into gold when I could turn gold into gold?

My wealth increased.

And then the dark came.

✳

I was at my labour one day when I heard terrible noises coming from the lower laboratory where Elizabeth worked. I ran to the door; it was locked. I begged her to open it, but she would not. I went upstairs, took an axe and broke down the door. Elizabeth was there, slumped at the table, blood streaming down her arm. There was a smell of burning.

I ran to her – my loved one, my lover, my love – and saw a parchment and paper on the desk. She was still and quiet. I did not know if she was faint or dead. I took some water and roused her.

'I have sold my Soul,' she said. 'I have signed in blood.'

The following day she left the house on Bankside and took a splendid lodging in Vauxhall by the Pleasure Gardens. She had a number of young men and women living there with her. Every night there were parties and revels. Every day the house was closed and silent.

I called on her many times but her servants had been instructed not to admit me. I had no idea where her money had come from and I assumed she had become the mistress of a lord or a duke.

I never believed what she had said about her Soul.

And then John Dee came briefly back to London.

By this time the laboratory had been left empty. We had both abandoned the Great Work. John Dee came to see me and it is true I felt ashamed because all of this was through him – my chance at life had been through him.

'Do you suppose,' he said, 'that the work was about gold, that it was about fancy stuffs such as magenta dyes? Do you not suppose it was about the Soul?'

'I do not know about the Soul,' I said. 'We are required to live as we must while we can.'

'Do you believe in God?'

'I don't think I do.'

John Dee nodded. 'Do you believe in the life to come?'

'I don't think I do.'

'Yet you have seen many strange things with me, have you not? Apparitions, spectres, unaccountable sights not of human form?'

'I think these things are the magick of our own minds, not visitations from elsewhere.'

'Then our minds must be multitudes indeed.'

'I think we are worlds compressed into human form.'

John Dee looked at me and smiled. 'Worlds compressed into human form. I like it that you say that. Whatever you are you are not the pragmatist I feared. And I believe that you will guard the secrets that you know – our secrets of alchemy and great intent?'

I told him I was trustworthy and he said he had always thought it so. Then his face clouded. 'Elizabeth. I cannot save her. She has taken the Left-Hand Path.'

'Do you say that there is a Devil – pitchfork, hooves, Hell – who has taken her Soul? Do you say that?'

'The Dark Gentleman has neither pitchfork nor hooves but he is Lord of Hell.'

✱

That night I wrote a letter to Elizabeth begging her to see me.

The Net

Christopher Southworth was on his feet. There was a commotion in the courtyard outside the window. Alice looked out. She could see Harry Hargreaves talking angrily to her groom. His men had caught someone.

Christopher was pulling on his boots and fastening his dagger. She gave him a key. 'My study is locked. Stay out of sight until I come for you.'

Alice tied up her hair, put on a dressing gown, took up a candle.

As she was about to go, Christopher caught her arm. 'You said that time was 1582. That was thirty years ago, Alice. How old are you?'

She said nothing. She opened the door and went

downstairs. Her servants were in the hall. There was Constable Hargreaves and James Device.

'James! Have they caught you for poaching on my land?'

'He escaped armed guard at Malkin Tower,' said Hargreaves.

'I dreamed I was a hare and as a hare I ran away.'

'And what are you doing here, Jem?' said Alice.

Jem looked at Alice and said nothing. Hargreaves punched him in the stomach. He doubled up, winded. 'Looking for a place to hide.'

'And so you came to the Rough Lee?' said Hargreaves.

'Mistress Nutter will protect me.'

'And why would she protect the likes of you, you ditch-scum?'

Alice said, 'Constable Hargreaves, it is late at night. I am not responsible for your drunken guards who let this man escape, nor for his decision to come here. I have barns and stables where he thought he might hide, and I am patron in charity to the Demdike. That is all. Now leave.'

'He came to you . . .' repeated Hargreaves. 'He might have gone anywhere to hide, but he came to you.' He punched Jem again.

Jem turned to Alice, hunted as the hare he dreamed himself to be. 'Help me,' he said.

'I cannot help you, Jem,' said Alice.

'Take him away,' said Constable Hargreaves. 'Lock his legs this time.'

Gradually the noises of the men were silenced into the dark and the last of the flares disappeared into the hill. Alice went back inside and sent the servants to bed. Then she went to her study and brought out Christopher Southworth. He had heard it all. He took Alice by her shoulders.

'Alice – they were hunting me and found him. I like none of this. The net is tightening and you do not feel it. Jem Device or some other of his demented kin will accuse you of witchcraft when they discover that you will not help them. You want to protect the Demdike but they will not protect you.'

'I have not told you the rest of my story.'

The Dark Gentleman

That night I wrote a letter to Elizabeth begging her to see me . . .

The following day a servant came to me and asked if I would wait upon his mistress that night at her house in Vauxhall. It was Maytime, Beltane, and the full moon.

At sunset, as I had been instructed, I went to her house and dismissed my servant.

I could hear a great noise coming from the hall that was placed in the centre of the house. I entered and saw a large company of men and women unknown to me. All wore masks across the eyes. Some wore animal tails. I was not announced, nor was I given a mask. I walked freely around the room, looking for Elizabeth. There was a table piled with food and drink. Two fiddlers played.

A man in a mask kissed me. I pushed him away. He said, 'We are free spirits here.'

Suddenly Elizabeth came towards me. 'Alice! Tonight is our great ceremony of Beltane and I would that you were one of our company. You are rich but you could be richer yet. Your beauty will remain. Your power will increase. The Dark Gentleman has asked for you himself.'

I felt a chill on me like the beginning of winter. I looked across the room and there was a small handsome man staring at me with deep black eyes. He bowed briefly as I looked at him.

Elizabeth laughed. 'Here is no simple charm. Here is everlasting power.'

She kissed me fully. She drew me aside to a small room off the hall. We had undressed in moments and made love like wolves.

But while she was touching me I felt something strange about her left hand. I pulled it up from my body. The third finger of her left hand was missing.

'I married the Dark Gentleman,' she said. 'The

Christians give a ring. The Dark Lord takes a finger.'

I folded her fingers. Kissed them. 'You belong to me,' I said.

She shook her head. 'I did once upon a time, but you never belonged to me, did you, Alice? You gave me your body but you never gave me your Soul.'

I touched her face. Her green eyes were full of tears. And yet she was different, changed. She was as beautiful as ever but her softness was gone. She was bright like something from the sea, like treasure that the sea has covered in coral.

She wore a simple gold ring on her little finger. She took it off, put it on the third finger of my left hand. My hands are smaller than hers. 'Remember me,' she said.

I looked at her. She was my memory. There was no one else to remember.

'Now,' she said, 'you will be one of us. Come.'

She threw me a silk petticoat and took my hand. We went back into the hall.

There had been a change. A table covered with a red cloth stood on a dais. On the table were four black candles, lit, giving off a foul stink. 'Sulphur and pitch,' whispered Elizabeth. 'Come forward.'

I went forward, realising that while I was wearing only a shift, the others in their masks were fully clothed. My heart was beating too fast.

A figure came towards me offering a drink in a silver cup. I took it and drained it off. Everyone in the room was clapping. They stamped their feet as the fiddle music got wilder and discordant. Elizabeth was holding my hand. 'The Dark Gentleman will make you his own.'

Without understanding what I did I took off my shift. I was naked now. The Dark Gentleman walked forward, picked me up with surprising strength so that my legs were wrapped round his waist while he had intercourse with me. I was heady with the drink and with my pleasure with Elizabeth and I enjoyed him.

I saw that others in the room were now at the same business, half naked and hungry for each other. All the time the music played.

While I was still at my pleasure, I saw Elizabeth put on a fur cloak and make her way to the door to the street. Why was she leaving without me?

The crowd parted. A shape – I cannot call it a figure – moved – I cannot call it walked – through the bodies. The shape carried a sword. The shape was draped and hooded.

The Dark Gentleman had finished with me. I leaned back against the altar. From far away I heard Elizabeth's voice. 'She is the One.'

The Wound

Christopher Southworth was silent. He took Alice's hands and kissed them. 'I met you at Salmsbury Hall when I was a boy. What was I? Eighteen? I fell in love with you. I became a priest. I remained in love with you. Whatever you are, I will always love you.'

Alice touched his chest. He pulled his shirt over his head. His chest was stamped with scars from the branding iron and the red-hot wires. She stroked his scars. She did not flinch.

He kissed her forehead. 'I will always love you but I can't be your lover.'

'God will forgive you.'

'I have nothing for Him to forgive.'

He unbuttoned his breeches and taking Alice's hand laid it against his groin.

They had taken the Jesuit Christopher Southworth to a cell without windows. In the cell was a rack, a winch, a furnace, a set of branding irons, a pot for melting wax, nails of different lengths. A thumbscrew, a pair of flesh-tongs, heavy tweezers, a set of surgical instruments, a series of small metal trays, ropes, wire, preparations of quicklime, a hood and a blindfold.

They did not rack him but they used the rack as a bench. They tied his arms above his head, legs apart. They made a small neat cut in his side and drained a quart of blood to weaken him. Then they forced him to drink a pint of salt water.

They did not break his fingers joint by joint or pull out his teeth one by one. They were relaxed. They drew pictures on his chest with their delicate knives, carefully cleaning the blood away. They pinned back his eyelids with metal clips and dripped hot wax into his eyeballs. When he screamed they debated whether or not to take out his tongue. But they wanted his tongue for his confession.

He did not confess. He gave them no names. The only name they heard was Jesus.

He was naked. They stroked his penis and his balls. To his shame his penis hardened. He felt nothing but he hardened. The men were excited by him. They turned him over and buggered him. They turned him back and prepared a small fire in a tin. Then while one of the men held his penis the other cut it off. Then they cut off his balls. He had fainted but they threw water over him and roused him. They burned his testicles in the small tin. He couldn't see anything but he could smell himself. The stench of himself. Burning alive. Then they left him alone.

He said, 'There is a ship that sails from Dover in fifteen days. Be on it. Be on it with me.'

'What about my house? My land?'

'What about your life?'

'My life is not in danger. Yours is.'

'I no longer care about my life. I died when they tortured me – or so it feels.'

She undressed him. She kissed him. Gently he divided her legs with his hands and moved down the bed so that his tongue could reach her.

They both fell asleep.

A Life for a Life

Constable Hargreaves unlocked the leg irons and took James Device round the corner to the Dog.

Tom Peeper was there in the dark low-fired room. A naked half-asleep child sat on his knee. She pulled her dress on over her head and ran off without speaking to her brother. Tom Peeper stood up and fastened his breeches.

'How did she get out of the Tower?' said Hargreaves.

'I locked 'em in. I let 'em out,' said Peeper. 'Not that sly toad I didn't though.' He gave Jem a kick. 'Devil must have let you out.'

Jem looked like an animal at the food and drink.

He stretched out his hand. 'You've had my sister. Give me beer and bread.'

He tried to snatch the crust but Tom Peeper slapped him aside.

'She's not yours to trade, Jem, not now, property of the Law. That right, Harry?'

Harry Hargreaves said nothing. He had no appetite for the children Tom used but he wouldn't stop him using them. Tom Peeper was useful. He was a spy and a sadist. That made Hargreaves's job easier.

'We'll give you food, Jem,' said Hargreaves. 'Eat up.'

Jem hesitated, but only for a second. He sat on the bench, both elbows on the table and shoved food into his mouth with both hands. He drank with his mouth full, slopping and choking, scooping up the slushy mess that fell out of his mouth. He ate unconcerned for anything, except his food, as a man who is often starving eats. Peeper glanced over at Hargreaves. They had worked together for a long time. They had an understanding.

'There's a dungeon for you, Jem, in Lancaster. Makes the Malkin Tower look like a royal palace. Your grand-dam hasn't escaped and neither will you, not as a hare, not as a bird, and not with a league of Dark Gentlemen to escort you. You will leave on a cart and you will be burned at the stake.'

Jem ate steadily, without looking up, but he was listening.

'You could save yourself. Testify against your kin and they will burn and you will be free. We'll send you away quietly. Roger Nowell will get you a billet in Yorkshire. You'll have food to eat, clothes to wear, a barn to sleep in, a fire in winter. You can get married. How about that, Jem? A wife to keep you warm. Something better than your squinty mother or a greasy sheep to quieten your cock. All you have to do is to confess to Roger Nowell that the meeting at Malkin Tower was a band of witches. A blasphemous Good Friday plot. We will not remember the stolen sheep or any other thing against you.'

Jem was eating and thinking. Eating was easy. Thinking was hard. They were only asking him to tell the truth. He saw a picture in his head of the straw bed in the barn and the chicken in the pot and his sweetheart working in the fields, and her coming home in the evening and them being together, away from all this forever.

'And you would testify against Alice Nutter.'

Jem stopped eating and dreaming. His face was full of fear. He shook his head. 'I may not speak against her.'

Tom Peeper put his nose in very close. 'Why may you not speak against her? What power has she over you?'

Jem shook his head again. 'I will be torn in quarters by demons.'

Tom Peeper took up the smoky dripping candle and held back Jem's head. 'I can quarter you faster today than any devil tomorrow. And where I am too soft and silly, the torturer at Lancaster will make up for my slackness.' He dashed the hot wax into Jem's face.

Jem jumped away and went whimpering into the corner of the room. There was a big spider on the floor. The spider said, 'James Device, I will protect you. Do what they ask and I will make you greater than she.'

'Are you a fiend?' said Jem.

'I am your friend, James Device. Put me in your pocket and listen to me carefully.'

'Get up off the floor, you length of rotten rope!' shouted Peeper.

Jem pocketed the spider and stood up. 'I will testify against them all.'

Constable Hargreaves refilled the tankards. 'And what of Mistress Nutter?'

Jem took his beer and drained it off. 'I will say to Magistrate Nowell that she promised to lead us and to blow up the gaol at Lancaster and free Old Demdike.'

He started to laugh – high, hysterical. They were laughing with him. He wasn't alone and outside any more. Not cold or hungry or afraid. He would be safe now.

The Hell Hole

The Well Dungeon at Lancaster Castle measures twenty feet by twelve feet. It is sunk thirty feet below ground. It has no window and no natural light, save for a grille, slotted into the floor at ground level, but ground level is thirty feet above. Might as well be the moon away. And the moon looks in at night, high and pale, a cold light, but on full moon a light at least.

And better than the fat-drenched flare that drips its pig grease onto the filthy straw and lights up . . . what does it light up? Misery, emaciation, rot, suffering, rats.

The prisoners are not chained. They roam around their stall. Chattox paces like a show cat, back and forth, forth and back, muttering nobody knows what. Her daughter, pretty Nance Redfern, sits in the corner hating Alizon Device, her rival for food and a few brief hours out of this hell. The gaoler takes one or the other for sex most days. He washes them too, or at least the part that interests him. Therefore the two young women have fewer sores than the rest.

The place stinks. Drainage is a channel cut into the earth under the straw. Their urine flows away, their faeces pile into a corner. Old Demdike squats over the mounting pile and generally loses her footing and slips into it. Her dress is smeared in excrement. She has weeping sores between her legs. When the gaoler comes for one of the women, Demdike lifts her dress and leers at him, offering him her sores. He hits her. She has lost two teeth this way.

They are fed stale bread and brackish water twice a day. When the bread is thrown through the door, the rats squeal at it and have to be kicked away. There are four or five rats. There were more. The rest have been eaten.

Cold. The dungeon is cold and the women have only a couple of horse blankets to share between them. When it rains, the rain falls through the grating and soaks the straw underneath. Jane Southworth stands under the rain chute and tries to wash her face and hands, tries to wash between her legs, and the others laugh at her, but the rain is liquid sanity to her. It comes from outside and she tries to imagine that some of the outside enters this hellish inside and makes it bearable.

The wet straw adds to the smell of rot.

The walls have moss on them and strange dark fungus. Demdike knows her toadstools and scrapes what she can from the walls. The heavy iron manacles hung round the walls are rusted. When she has the fit on her, Demdike shakes the manacles with all her strength calling for her Familiar to come and save her. Greymalkin never comes, nor the small gentleman dressed in black that she used to know, nor the brown imp that lived in a bottle, nor the bird that told her where the grain was kept. Nothing human or not human enters this place. The gaoler never comes in and when the women are questioned they are called to come out by name. Every kind of disease is in these walls.

It is April. The women will be here until the August Assizes.

Chattox and Demdike hate each other. Their daughters Nance and Alizon hate each other. No alliances have been made. No sympathy each to each. Jane Southworth keeps herself apart. She recites the Bible and that enrages the others.

He will come, says Old Demdike, one night, on a moon-trail, he will come and I'll be rid of the lot of you.

At first the rival families made spells and invocations. At first fire and blood were used to lure the Dark Gentleman. Now there are curses but no hope. Misery but no invention. Alizon wonders about Old Demdike's power. Demdike swears he will come but she no longer believes it.

Day and night are the same. Fitful cold aching sleep, pain, thirst, tiredness even when asleep.

The straw moves underfoot with lice.

The air is stagnant. Breathing is hard because the air is so thick. Too much carbon dioxide. Not enough oxygen. Every breath keeps them alive and kills them off some more. One of the women has a fever.

The door opens. The gaoler is there with a dripping flare.

'Nance!' he shouts, and shoves the flare in the socket. He leaves them light while he takes the woman; it is his way of signalling something . . . what?

The flare throws grotesque shadows on the black stone walls of the cell. No, it is not the shadows that are grotesque; the women are grotesque. Shrunken, stooped, huddled, crippled, hollow-faced, racked and rattling.

Alizon uses her hands to make a play-theatre. Here is a rabbit. Here is a bird. Old Demdike sways back and forth in her soiled dress.

It is raining a little, and Jane Southworth goes to her station under the grille, opening her mouth to the rain. She lets the rain on her face be her tears. None of the women cry any more.

She thinks about Hell, and is it like this? She thinks that the punishments of the Fiend are made out of human imaginings. Only humans can know what it means to strip a human being of being human. She thinks the Fiend has a kind of purity that humans never have. She thinks that godliness is ridiculous because it exists to hide this; this stinking airless doomed cell. Life is a stinking airless doomed cell. Why do we pretend? She can smell strawberries. She knows she is going mad. Let the rain come.

A rat runs over her foot and drinks from the indent of her shoe.

Hoghton Tower

Alice Nutter and Roger Nowell were riding ahead of their group. Alice said nothing about Constable Hargreaves or Jem Device or the events of the previous night. When Roger Nowell enquired after his fashion if she had slept well, she said she had. She hoped he had found his fugitive. He had not.

Potts was travelling with them. He was a poor rider and preferred a carriage, but roads in Lancashire were not so necessary as they were in London, and so Potts had to be content with bouncing along the ruts and bridleways in an open cart drawn by a farmer's nag. He was bad-tempered enough from a night without sleep and not a single broomstick to be seen on Pendle Hill. He had been curious to meet Alice Nutter but she made him nervous. Something about the way she looked at him made him feel less important than he knew himself to be.

He was glad to be travelling behind the mounted party.

Roger Nowell was glad of it too. He and Alice were both distracted by their own thoughts and said little to one another.

Alice had woken well before dawn. Christopher was sleeping next to her, sleeping heavily like a man who has not slept enough for a long time, sleeping carelessly, on his back, his arm thrown out, like a child who is safe.

She had made him get up, taken him down the secret passageway between her bedroom and her study. Locked him in. Left him. She did not know if she would see him again. He wanted to leave for Lancaster. She knew that she loved him.

'Hoghton Tower,' said Roger Nowell, pausing his

horse and breaking her thoughts. 'It is a splendid house.'

They had reached the mile-long drive that led to the house. The de Hoghtons had come to England with William the Conqueror, but this house, fifty years old, had been built by Thomas Hoghton, who had scarcely been able to enjoy it. He would not renounce his Catholic faith and had been forced to flee to France.

'He was harbouring Edmund Campion,' said Roger Nowell. 'Remember him?'

Alice remembered. 'Burned alive for his faith.'

'Thomas Hoghton was lucky to escape himself. He used his money to found the Jesuit Seminary at Douai in France,' said Roger Nowell. 'Christopher Southworth trained as a priest there.'

Alice glanced across at him, but his face was straight ahead, admiring the house.

'Hoghton's son Richard has no heart for religion but a good nose for politics. Consequently he has kept the house and good King Scottish Jimmy gave him a knighthood last year.'

'Are you not fond of our King James?' said Alice.

'He is a meddler, and when the King is a meddler, the rest of us must be meddlers too. Do you think I enjoy sending old women and their crazed offspring to the gallows?'

'Then do not ask me to help you.'

'Then do not ask *me* to help *you*, Mistress.'

He dropped his horse back a little, leaving her to ride ahead. He could not help noticing her figure, her posture, her hair, the quality of her beauty. He had never been interested in her before. He checked himself. This was not the time.

Alice Nutter was dressing in her room. She was careful to look her best. Her maid fastened her magenta dress and hung her neck and her ears with emeralds. When the maid had gone, Alice took a small phial from her bag and wiped her face with a few drops. There was not much left in the stoppered bottle. John Dee had made it and given it to Alice. It was not the Elixir of Life but it was the Elixir of Youth.

She came downstairs to find Potts talking to a

small, balding, genial man. 'As a London gentleman I find these country entertainments very tedious,' said Potts.

'Then why attend them?' asked the owlish man.

'I am a guest of Magistrate Nowell. I am in Lancashire on matters of the Crown. Yes, the Crown,' said Potts, fluffing himself up. 'I may say nothing, but you would hardly believe the witchery popery popery witchery I have uncovered.'

'You must be exhausted,' said Alice, joining the two men. 'You look exhausted.'

The genial gentleman smiled at her. Potts glared. A bell rang. A servant announced the start of the play.

'Shakespeare,' said Potts. 'An upstart crow. Melodramatic and mediocre. *Macbeth* — that was a ridiculous play. And to my mind very suspicious too.'

'Suspicious?'

'The foul hags, witches, beldames, prophesying to Macbeth — do they not have "the pilot's thumb" to throw in their infernal pot?'

'They do . . .'

'Aha! And that is the thumb of Edmund Campion, Jesuit burned for treason, harboured here in this house, oh yes, while Shakespeare himself was a tutor here.'

'And that means . . .?' said the genial gentleman, trying to follow.

'Witchery popery popery witchery – all the same thing.'

The genial gentleman shrugged and offered Alice his arm. 'May I escort you in to the play?'

Alice nodded, just as Roger Nowell came forward looking for her. He barely glanced at Potts. He bowed to Alice's companion.

'William Shakespeare.'

Potts was suddenly nowhere to be seen.

As they took their seats for the play, Alice and Shakespeare were talking. He had met her many years ago, he said, when he was new to London, just come from Stratford, and she had her house on Bankside by the Swan Theatre. She welcomed him like a northern woman. He liked northern women for their forthrightness and their kindness – he had met many of them when he was a young man here at Hoghton Tower.

'We were all Catholics then,' he said, 'even when we were not.'

'Ah, we were young then,' said Alice.

Shakespeare looked at her curiously. 'Even when we were not.'

She blushed. He was like an owl, bright-eyed, his head perched on his ruff. His eyes looked deeper than his gaze and Alice felt that he knew everything and that there was nothing she need say.

He was a wealthy man now, living in Stratford, no longer writing plays. He had travelled up to see *The Tempest* at Hoghton Tower because he was fond of the place and fond of the play. His company was still the King's Men, and *The Tempest* had been chosen for the wedding of King James's daughter, to take place the following year.

'I have ridden out all the storms,' said Shakespeare, 'even the ones I wrote myself. Here, look, it begins . . .'

A tempestuous noise of thunder and lightning heard.
Enter a Shipmaster and a Boatswain.
MASTER: Boatswain!
BOATSWAIN: Here, master. What cheer?

Alice's mind moved in and out of the play. She remembered Shakespeare coming to her house – but he had had long hair, an earring, a beautiful beard. She had not recognised him this time.

As the play was performed, she seemed to hear Elizabeth's voice again – and they were together in the house on Bankside, upstairs in their secret private rooms that looked over the River Thames and across London, the great city.

'Did you sell your Soul, Lizzy?'

'The Dark Gentleman will take a Soul. It need not be my own.'

'I doubt another will go to Hell to pay for your pleasure.'

'You do not believe in Hell or Souls, do you, Alice?'

'I believe that you are changed.'

Alice looked up, startled from her dreaming by the stronger dreaming of the play.

ARIEL: Full fathom five thy father lies,
Of his bones are coral made:
Those are pearls that were his eyes:
Nothing of him that doth fade,
But doth suffer a sea-change
Into something rich and strange.

Alice fainted.

When she came to, she was in a small room away from the main hall. She could hear that the play was continuing. Her servant stood over her. William Shakespeare took the water from him and gave it to her. He said he was flattered that his little play had had such an effect on her.

She had got lost in time, she said. Time, he said, yes, yes, time was the kind of place where you could get lost.

Then she said to him, and she did not know why she said it, 'Do you believe in magick?'

'Why are you asking me, an actor and an old penman, when you worked with John Dee and Edward Kelley?'

'You knew them?'

'I knew anyone interesting to know. Tell me, do you think a stone statue can come to life? I have used that device in a play I am still revising called *The Winter's Tale*. The end cannot succeed unless you believe, just for a moment, that a statue could perhaps step down and embrace you. Return what you had lost.'

'John Dee made a metal beetle that flew like a living thing. He was arrested for it as sorcery.'

'You can get arrested for anything these days. But I don't think I can end my play with a metal beetle – however lifelike.'

'You haven't answered me,' said Alice.

Shakespeare shook his head and sunk his chin into his ruff, making him look more owl-like than ever. 'I have written about other worlds often enough. I have said what I can say. There are many kinds of reality. This is but one kind.' He stretched out his hands to indicate the walls, carpets, tapestries and stuffs around him. 'But, Mistress, do not be seen to stray too far from the real that is clear to others, or you may stand accused of the real that is clear to you.'

The door opened and Roger Nowell entered, with some of the party. Everyone was praising Shakespeare, except for Potts who was skulking in a corner. To Nowell he said, 'You do know, don't you, that this playwright, as he calls himself, this Shakespeare, was well known to Catesby, chief among the Gunpowder plotters?'

Roger Nowell nodded, irritated.

Potts continued: 'There were two buzzing hives of Catholics in England. A hive at Stratford-upon-Avon. A hive in Lancashire. All of the conspirators of the Gunpowder Plot met to make their plans at the Mermaid Inn in Stratford. Stratford, sir! Shakespeare sir! When the plot failed and they were routed, they fled, all of them, to Lancashire, hiding here at Hoghton Tower, or with the Southworths at Salmesbury Hall.'

'I know that,' said Roger Nowell.

'It astonishes me what you know and yet refuse to know. You fly near the edge, sir, near the edge.'

Alice, a little way off, stood up to leave the room. Potts regarded her. 'That lady is a mystery, sir, a mystery. If she were my mystery I would look deeper into it.'

'I am not as idle as you imagine,' replied Roger Nowell.

Alice went upstairs to her rooms to change her clothes. It was not yet dark, but it was not light: the Daylight Gate. And if you could pass through – to what – to where?

Alice lay down on the big bed with a single candle and the fire burning low. She closed the bed curtains and closed her eyes. She was beginning to fall asleep when she heard someone or something moving about in the room.

From the cabin of her bed what she could hear sounded like water.

Not rain, not river. The strange combination of

a being made of water. Something was treading about her room. Not as a solid – as a liquid.

Then she heard the sizzle and hiss of the wood in the fireplace as the fire was put out.

Her mouth dry; forcing herself to move, she swung out of bed and opened the bed curtains.

The room was not there.

Alice was standing on Pendle Hill. Black moor, bleak fell, straggling forest, sullen streams, a small tarn, a moss pool, heathy waste, morass and wood. Driving rain.

By a group of standing stones she saw Elizabeth Southern, her hair down, naked, smiling at her. Elizabeth was untroubled by the weather, pushing the hair out of her eyes as she used to do, seemingly not cold or wet. She stretched out her hand to Alice. Alice went towards her through the rain and the wind. If this was the end, then let it be the end, the end would come some time, today, tomorrow, or the next day.

Alice touched Elizabeth's naked body, but as her hand stroked the skin she had loved so much, the skin gave way, like soaked paper, and Alice's hand went through her, or, more correctly, into her. It was like reaching into black water.

Alice pulled back, her hand and arm dark and dull with the thick black viscous substance that was Elizabeth.

Elizabeth was laughing, and as she laughed, her white skin began to spot with dark eruptions. The firm white flesh became distended and pulpy. The eruptions burst like boils. Her hair turned grey, then loosened from her scalp, falling away from her like dirty water. The skin on her bones hung in useless folds. She had no teeth. She was laughing at Alice, her mouth like a gap. She was suppurating, liquefying.

'As I am so shall you be.'

Alice covered her face with her hands. She stood in the howling gale and relentless rain trying to keep upright. She would not look at Elizabeth.

'What do you want from me?' she shouted into the wind and the rain. There was no answer. Forever, it seemed, in the wind and the rain, and there was no answer.

Alice was crying. Then there was silence. A sick dead silence.

When she looked up, she was in her room. The fire was lit low. Everything was as it had been before.

She was soaking wet.

At supper that night Potts was regaling the company with his 'discovery' of a nest of Lancashire witches now under lock and key at Malkin Tower. Alice lost patience.

'There was no Sabbat – you stayed up all night on Pendle Hill and what did you find? Nothing! And nothing at Malkin Tower but a pack of desperate miserable spoiled lives.'

'You are heated in your defence,' said Potts, 'though their lair is on your land and they are under your protection –'

Shakespeare interrupted: 'What is a Black Mass? The rusty candlesticks and hasty altars you find in remote places, wild, and away from men, are the remnants of the Catholic High Mass, sometimes celebrated in secret, if it is to be celebrated at all.'

'You do not believe in witchcraft then?' said Roger Nowell.

'I did not say that. I say that it suits the times to degrade the *hoc est corpus* of the Catholic Mass into satanic hocus pocus.'

'It is all the same,' said Potts.

'It is not the same,' said Shakespeare.

'I wonder about your sympathies, sir,' said Potts, 'and you and your company of strolling players in receipt of the King's generosity.'

'We are the King's Men,' said Shakespeare. 'And besides – I began this play *The Tempest* with a shipwreck in sympathy with the King's own shipwreck by supernatural forces on his way back from Denmark to Berwick.'

'Ah, the Berwick witch trials,' said Potts. 'There has been nothing as sensational until now. The Lancashire witch trials will be the first trials to be written as record. A great advantage in the pursuit of Diabolism.'

'Are you doing the writing?' enquired Shakespeare.

'In my legal capacity, yes. I have written plays also, you know.'

'I didn't know,' said Shakespeare, 'neither does anybody else.'

The table roared with laughter. Potts looked red and angry. Alice was enjoying his discomfort.

'I wonder you dare venture out of doors in Lancashire for fear of meeting a witch or a priest,' said Alice.

'What do you mean by that?' said Roger Nowell, looking not at Potts but at Alice.

'Whatever she means,' said Shakespeare, 'this man's a fool.'

This was sufficient to drive Potts from the supper table. Roger Nowell laughed with the rest, but he was uneasy too. Potts had found no flying witches. He was looking for a hiding priest.

It was late and Alice was getting ready for bed when she heard a soft tap at the door. She opened it to find Shakespeare standing outside in his gown and slippers. He put his finger to his lips. She let him in.

'A word of advice from a man who has seen much. If you do not want to find yourself in the

Well Dungeon at Lancaster Castle, leave England soon. Christopher Southworth must go with you.'

'Why do you speak of him?'

'Take heed what you are told. Take heed what you tell.'

Shakespeare opened the door. He said, 'Oftentimes, to win us to our harm, the instruments of darkness tell us truths, win us with honest trifles to betray in deepest consequence.'

Alice did not sleep well. When she was ready to leave at the agreed hour of 9 a.m., she was told by a servant of the house that the fog was too thick and she and her party must wait until noon. Roger Nowell was nowhere to be found. Potts was dozing in the library.

She waited, restless, finally calling her maid, and going herself to order their horses. It was eleven o'clock. The groom who saddled her copper mare told her that Roger Nowell had ridden away unaccompanied at 6 a.m.

She had been tricked.

A Tooth for a Tooth

Roger Nowell and Constable Hargreaves were standing in the thick fog in the graveyard of Newchurch in Pendle. They looked down in silence. The turf had been flung back and the shallow earth disturbed. The body within was partially uncovered; bones showed in the earth and above ground. By the side of the grave was a skull, dry and bleached. The skull had been smashed at the jaw to remove the teeth. Bits of chipped bone were scattered about. The teeth had been carefully collected in a mound.

At another grave the ground had been re-dug but the body it held had not yet rotted to the bones and the mouldering flesh was exposed, with its busy colony of worms. The corpse had been mutilated. The head was gone, leaving only the black stump of the neck.

'Happened last night,' said Hargreaves. 'They made off with the head and left the teeth. Must have been disturbed at their work.'

'Aren't the Demdike and Chattox locked up?'

'All but James Device who is prepared to give evidence against his kin. He is dead drunk at the Dog.'

'Then we cannot blame him. And much as you would all like to do so, we cannot blame Alice Nutter. She was with me.'

'Her spirit can go abroad. The spirit of a witch can go abroad anywhere,' said Hargreaves.

Roger Nowell did not answer that. 'Did you search the Rough Lee?'

'We did. I have a servant in my pay now. We found no Christopher Southworth nor any sign or sighting of him. But we found this.'

Hargreaves pulled out a silver crucifix on a neckchain. 'In the bedchamber . . . In the bed.'

Roger Nowell looked at it closely. 'Does she use

it because she is secretly a Catholic or because she is secretly a witch? Does she kiss it or does she blaspheme it?' He put the heavy crucifix in his pocket. 'It is valuable evidence.'

'James Device says he will testify against Alice Nutter.'

Roger Nowell shook his head. 'His drunken word would not stand against a woman like Alice Nutter. And we have enough work to do, Hargreaves. I want the wretches in Malkin Tower brought to me this evening to make statements. Potts will be present, I am sure. And get these graves decently laid.'

'Yes, sir. And Alice Nutter?'

'I have said not yet.'

Hargreaves was not pleased but he could not argue.

The men walked slowly from the churchyard. Jennet Device, who had been watching them from the bushes, ran up to the open graves, scooped up the teeth in both hands and made off towards Malkin Tower.

An Eye for an Eye

The speediest way to take a man's life away by witchcraft is to make a Picture of Clay, like unto the shape of a person whom they mean to kill, and dry it thoroughly; and when they would have them to be ill in any one place more than another, then take a thorne or a pinne and prick it in that part of the Picture you would so have to be ill; and when you would have any part of the body to consume away, then take that part of the Picture and burne it. And when they would have the whole body to consume away, then take the remnant of the said Picture and burne it; and thereupon by that means, the Body shall die. The same can be wrought by means of a Doll or Poppet.

Elizabeth Device was in the cellar of Malkin Tower. She was tending a cauldron coming to the boil over a dirty fire. A rough altar, a pair of sulphurous candles and a skeleton still chained to where its owner's body had left it, completed the furnishings of the cellar.

Mouldheels was nearby, busily sewing the legs onto a headless doll.

There was a shout from outside. Elizabeth Device went across the cellar and dragged away a large stone from a small hole. Fast as a ferret, Jennet Device crawled through, a small cloth bag in her mouth.

Her mother emptied the bag of teeth onto the altar. She gave Jennet a scrap of bread. While her daughter was eating, Elizabeth unwrapped from a cloth the severed head from the graveyard. Then she laid out Robert Preston's tongue.

'Mouldheels! Sew the tongue into this head. The teeth are going into the pot. I have used everything. All of Demdike's stored arts must be used for the spell.'

'What do you do?' asked the child.

'What do I do? I'll tell you what I do. That poppet Mouldheels is finishing will serve to injure

Roger Nowell until he cries for mercy. We have no clay but we have rags enough to make a doll like your grandmother showed you, didn't she? With the pins and the thorns?'

The child nodded.

'And we will cause this severed head to speak. A spirit will speak through it and guide us.'

Mouldheels had the grisly half-rotted head on her knee. 'Jennet! Hold open this mouth while I do my sewing.'

Jennet came and pulled open the slack blue mouth of the corpse-head. 'There's a worm in there, Auntie.'

Mouldheels looked. 'Worms everywhere, poppet, we live as best we may in a world of worms, but wait till this good head speaks.'

Elizabeth was back at her pot. 'Jem didn't come back. You seen him, Jennet?'

The child looked away. 'He was frightened in the churchyard. He left the teeth.'

'Where did he go, Jennet?'

The child shrugged and concentrated on the damp empty sockets of the head. Mouldheels was sewing the tongue to what was left of the roof of the mouth by making big stitches through what was left of the nose. 'Not much to anchor my line here,' she said. 'Lucky we had a fresh tongue. The tongue rots first. And the eyes o'course.'

'What is the pot for, Ma?'

'Nothing to eat if you were thinking it so. When the head is ready we shall boil it in the pot and then we shall boil the doll in the pot so that our spell is good on both.'

'What did you put in it? Sheep brain?'

'No, child. I made the sacrifice and used the baby in the bottle.'

The child Jennet let out a great wail, so much so that the trapdoor above was pulled back for a second and someone called to see what was the harm.

'That was my toy.'

'It was your toy, I know it well, and I had to smash the bottle to get the baby out, but she will set us all free and give us power and then you will get another toy as much as you like,'

'I shall have nowt to talk to now the baby is boiled.'

'You will talk to the Head, my dearie, and the Head will talk to you. The baby couldn't talk, could she?'

Tears running down her filthy face, Jennet shook her head. She was a sad sight, dirty and torn and bruised, her blonde hair in knots, her skin calloused from crawling and hiding. 'I gived you the tongue of Robert Preston from under the bush. You said you'd give me something for it.'

'And I will!' said her mother. 'Soon all this will change.'

Mouldheels had finished her gruesome sewing. The swollen black tongue protruded from the mouth cavity of the head.

She plunged the head into the stew. The cauldron boiled over in a sickening froth.

Mouldheels came forward and taking the doll she had made, she pierced it through with a sharp stick and baptised it in the cauldron: '*In his likeness it is moulded, he shall die.*' And she plunged the doll under the scummy water. It shrieked.

Elizabeth pushed Mouldheels aside, and with a pair of heavy tongs she fished in the boiling brew for the head, lifted it out and set it to drain. Much of what had remained of the decomposing flesh had been scalded off into the pot. The head retained a few strands of hair and its new tongue. It sat on the altar, steaming as the water fell from it.

The stench in the cellar was so bad that the company assembled above began to complain. Elizabeth got on the wormy ladder and poked her head into the room. 'When you are free and Roger Nowell is dead you will not complain. And when we are free we shall fly to Lancaster Castle where the Dark Gentleman will reward us for our pains.'

'We cannot do it without Old Demdike or without Mistress Nutter,' said one.

But Elizabeth was blazing now. 'I have claimed the power. I shall lead you. My proof will be the proof of my Spell.' She went back down into her lair. 'Mouldheels, bring up the head.'

Mouldheels took a cloth and wrapped the damp head in it. Elizabeth climbed the ladder into the round room of Malkin Tower and reached down for the head. As it was produced, the company gasped.

'Yea,' said Elizabeth, 'now you see me. I have made the head that not even Demdike could make. The head will speak to you, confirm my power, and guide us from this place.'

She placed the head on the plank-board table.

'At sunset it will speak. In Demdike's name it will speak.'

In the cellar Jennet Device was poking in the cauldron for the remains of her bottled baby. She found a tiny hand and put it carefully in her dress pocket.

The Fog

Alice Nutter had ridden home to the Rough Lee to discover that Roger Nowell had ordered her house to be searched. She was sitting in her study with Christopher Southworth. He kept fingering his neck. She made a joke about the noose. He shook his head. 'I have lost my crucifix. I took it off in your bed. Now I cannot find it. I took it off to make love to you.'

She kissed him as they sat either side of the fire. She had made up her mind. 'I will leave for France with you, Kit.'

He looked at her in disbelief. She stood up. 'I dreamed of Elizabeth Southern last night, if it was a dream – a nightmare. For the first time in a long time I feel afraid. It is as if she is coming for me.'

'Coming for you? From beyond the grave?'

'Or near to it.' Alice was crying. Christopher tried to comfort her but she pulled away.

'That night I told you about, at Elizabeth Southern's house in Vauxhall, when I heard her voice say "She is the One". I had no doubt that I was to be a sacrifice, though I did not know what kind of sacrifice.'

A hooded figure advanced towards me. I picked up the two candles made of sulphur and pitch. I hurled them into the dreadful shape. The robes of the creature caught fire. Those in the room shrank back. This gave me courage. I ran sideways towards the door. I reached the door; it was locked and barred. The crowd was on me and the fearful figure burning towards me.

I stripped off my shift and set it alight from a wall-torch. Now there were two of us burning. I swung my burning shift in front of me, making a fiery barrier between myself and the crowd. One grabbed it and burned his hand. Another tried to slip behind me but I hit him in the face with the flaming garment.

There was a window behind me leading directly onto the street. I backed up to it, turned, and jumped straight out. My skin was scorched. My hair was on fire. I ran down to the Thames and threw myself in. I swam upstream like a burning mermaid until I was at Bankside. I scrambled out on a low pier and fell half drowned into my house.

John Dee was waiting for me.

He tended my burns with salve. He put me to bed. He looked at me gravely. 'Born in Fire. Warmed by Fire. By Fire to depart.'

'What are you saying?'

'Your nativity. You were born under the sign of Sagittarius. You are born in fire. That is the first part of the prophecy. You have studied the alchemical arts and so you have been warmed by fire. That is the second part of the prophecy. The third part of the prophecy is how you will die. Choose your own death or fire will choose you.'

'I do not understand what you say.'

'Elizabeth has betrayed you. She sold her Soul

to enjoy her wealth and power for a fixed time. Now, unless there is a substitute for her Soul, she will lose everything. You are the substitute.'

'I do not believe in those things.'

'It does not matter what you believe. Believe what is.'

John Dee stood up and brought over a mirror. It was a mirror I had made using mercury. It offered a surface reflection, like all mirrors, but behind the reflection was a deep view, like a magenta pool.

'Why do you think you look so youthful, Alice? You are almost forty years old.'

'It is true that I seem to have become younger since I met you.'

John Dee nodded. 'Mercurius is a youthful spirit. In the alchemical work he is the renewing force.'

'Then is it the mercury I have been using?'

John Dee shook his head. 'Only in part. I have experimented with an elixir. It is the elixir that I have instructed you to wipe over your entire body once a month at the new moon.'

'And Elizabeth too. Is that the secret of her beauty?'

'Elizabeth's beauty is dropping from her body like a ragged coat. She has failed to make you the sacrifice in her place. Look in the mirror – already she is ageing and withering.'

I looked in the mirror – her skin like parchment stretched over her face. Written on the body was disease, disfigurement, death.

Christopher Southworth sat up. 'Alice, who is Elizabeth Southern?'

'Southern was her own name. She married a man named Device. Elizabeth Southern is Old Demdike.'

Damn You

Roger Nowell was in pain. It began about noon as he finished his dinner and got up from the table. His legs buckled under him. He felt a sharp pain like a knife in his groin. He had to grab the edge of the oak table to stop himself falling. He called a servant who helped him up the stairs to bed. The doctor could not attend at once, and so the herbalist from Whalley was summoned. By the time she arrived Roger Nowell was in a bloodshot fever.

'I am being stabbed,' he said, 'run through with sharp irons.' He screamed and grabbed his chest as another searing pain tore through him.

The herbalist undid his shirt. She rolled back the blankets to look at his legs. His body looked as if it had been stabbed and stabbed. There were red marks all over him. The marks bled.

'This is not a natural ague,' said the herbalist. 'It is witchcraft.'

'Demdike,' said Roger Nowell. 'Damn her to Hell.'

Potts burst into the room looking triumphant. 'I have sensational news! Christopher Southworth is in Lancashire. Christopher Southworth is at the Rough Lee.'

'I know,' said Roger Nowell.

'You know? And you do nothing?'

'There is nothing to be done. I have had the house searched from top to bottom. No sign of the man.'

'Arrest Mistress Nutter.'

'I cannot arrest a woman for harbouring a man who is not there.'

'He is there!' shouted Potts, stamping his foot.

'I am ill,' said Roger Nowell.

Potts came over to the bed. He could see that Roger Nowell was indeed ill. 'This is sorcery!' said Potts.

'Demdike,' said Roger Nowell. 'I have ordered the crew from Malkin brought here this evening. If I am still alive I shall take witness statements.'

'I shall do all of that,' cried Potts, sensing his hour of glory approaching. 'And although you are struck down by witchcraft, why do you call on the Demdike for the offence? I will wager this is the work of Alice Nutter.'

The herbalist was offended. 'Mistress Nutter is skilled in the alchemical arts and knows her plants and powders but she is no witch and I will swear to it.'

'You will swear to nothing unless you want to join her at the stake,' said Potts.

The herbalist did not reply. She mixed up a potion and ordered Roger Nowell to drink it down. He did so and fell straight asleep.

The herbalist warned his manservant that he must not be disturbed until he woke naturally. Then she took her donkey and rode to the Rough Lee.

The Net Tightens

The fog was white at the window.

'Make your escape,' Alice said to Christopher Southworth. 'I have a hundred pounds here. Take it. I shall bring more in jewels. I shall send a chest to a trustworthy friend in London. We shall have linens and silver.'

She got up and went to her corner cupboard. 'This is the key to my house on Bankside. It is tenanted but I keep a room there that no one may enter. Give them this signet ring and show them this key.'

She gave him the things. 'When will you come?' he said.

'I will follow you tomorrow.'

He kissed her. He took her face in his hands. 'I love you.'

Alice looked out. The house and estate were as silent and empty as the fog. 'I shall bring you a horse. When you hear me at the window, jump down.'

Alice went out to the stables. The grooms were in the kitchen at this hour, eating, keeping warm. They had no instructions and the horses had been attended to. Alice saddled up a bay hunter. Bending down and lifting his hooves she fitted little cloth bags, one on each hoof, and led him softly and unheard to the side of the house.

Christopher was leaning out of the window, but the fog was so thick that he did not see her until she was directly underneath. He slung his bottles of water and wine across his body, checked his dagger, fastened his cloak. His hand went to his neck. Where was his crucifix?

But there was no time. He swung through the stone mullion window and dropped easily to the ground. Alice held the horse while he mounted. 'Do not be delayed,' he said. 'I am afraid.'

She did not answer. She leaned forward and kissed his hand. He rode the hunter slowly and silently through the gates. When he was clear, he took off the hoof-pads and set off at a trot. The fog was his friend. He knew the way.

Alice did not go back indoors. She walked round the side of the house to a bare seat under a still-bare apple tree, its branches hesitating into leaf. She sat down and put her head in her hands, glad of the heavy quiet of the fog.

She knew she had to gather her documents of leasehold and freehold. She had a cache of silver. It would take her a week to get to the outskirts of London. She would ride to Preston, sell her horse and take the coach to Manchester. In Manchester she would become someone else, and as someone else, she would make her way to London.

She was thinking all this when her falcon flew like a ghostly spirit into the apple tree. As she sat, she became aware of something falling into her lap, and then another something, and another something. Something like pebbles.

She picked up one of the droppings. It was not a pebble; it was a human tooth.

On With It

At Malkin Tower Elizabeth Device and Old Mouldheels had strung up the poppet of Roger Nowell. His legs were full of pins.

The band were growing restless. They had sat in a circle in front of the suppurating head waiting for it to speak. It had not spoken.

From the slits in the walls of the tower they could see the guards. The light was fading. The Daylight Gate.

'I say we break out of here, attack the guards,' said Agnes Chattox. 'We have a meathook and a pitchfork.'

'I tell you Roger Nowell is cast into his bed and will not rise.'

'If he rises before the moon none of us shall see the sun again.'

'I tell you he will be dead by nightfall. I tell you the head will speak.'

'If the head does not speak before Master Nowell, none here shall speak again.'

More

'These teeth,' said the herbalist, 'are from the fresh-robbed graves at Newchurch in Pendle. You have not heard?'

'I was at Hoghton.'

'A lurid venture. Head, bones, teeth, scraped out of a grave like worms from a barrel.'

'The Demdike are locked up.'

'If they are at Malkin, they are not locked up. There is a way out.'

'It is on my land. There is no way out of that tower.'

'No way out but through,' said the herbalist. 'I tell you Jennet Device was in the Dog last night with Tom Peeper, and James Device is more cunning than you think him.'

'Even if Jennet and Jem robbed the graves, they could not deliver their bag of rot to Malkin.'

'Certainly they could. I'll warrant it was Jennet took the brimming head, severed and wormy, and rolled it like a pig's bladder through the hole.'

'What hole?'

The herbalist put her head in her hands.

'And for what purpose?'

'A spell! Are you mad? Have you lost your wits? I swear they have sewn a poppet and charmed it and stabbed its legs. The teeth are for the pain. God knows – and I cross myself, though it be the old religion – what they stirred into that Devil's brew!'

'No!' said Alice. 'We are old friends but you are superstitious and I am not. Roger Nowell rode hastily in a damp dawn; that is all there is to it. He may believe it is witchcraft. That does not mean that it is.'

'Alice, I believe it *is* witchcraft. Roger Nowell believes it is witchcraft. The name he spoke was Demdike and then that little trumped-up man come for the Assizes –'

'Potts.'

'Potts said your name.'

'Mine?'

'Alice! You sent the poor fool Robert Preston to me with his tongue bit out, and all the gossip is that you sided with the Demdike cat who did the biting. Stood between a witch and a ducking is what is said at the Dog. I drink there. I hear things. I hear your name too often now. If Roger Nowell does not recover you will be the one to blame.'

'This is not about witchery.'

'Alice, I know you are hiding the priest. I am not the only one who whispers it.'

'He is gone,'

'Good.'

'What would you have me do?'

'Go to Malkin. Discover the enchanted poppet. Destroy it before Roger Nowell dies.'

The Spider Speaks

At the Dog, James Device was locked in an upstairs bedroom. He did not care. He was fed and he had somewhere to sleep out of the April rain.

Jem sat on the window seat in the bare room with its straw pallet bed. He wasn't used to being alone unless he was poaching in the forest, and in the forest you never were alone. There were other creatures looking for food too. Jem was friend to the otter and the badger, the fox and the rabbit, and if he had to trap a rabbit or snatch fish from the otter, that did not make them any less his companions. He knew the trees too, and leaned against them with his troubles and sometimes his happiness. He had not been happy for a long time.

He felt in his pocket. There was the spider.

She was a big spider, about the size of the palm of his hand. He looked at her. He liked her beady eyes and bristled legs. He stroked her black body. She carried a sac of eggs.

'James Device,' said the spider, 'tonight you must make full confession of the crimes of your grand-dam, your mother and your sisters.'

'But not little Jennet.'

'But Alice Nutter.'

'And then I will be free forever, won't I?'

The spider waved two of her legs. Jem thought she was waving for freedom.

'I will find thee a nook that will serve as support for a web and I will hang a bat nearby as a feast for you. You may eat him alive and use his leather wings for flight of your own. A spider that is not a fly yet can fly.' He laughed at his own wit.

'James Device,' said the spider, 'run away.'

'Run away? But what about my reward?'

'I have given you my advice,' said the spider.

'You told me to confess! You told me you

would protect me! You told me I should be greater than Alice Nutter.'

'Eight legs could not carry you fast enough away,' said the spider.

Save Me

Tom Peeper and Constable Hargreaves finished drinking at the Dog and set off towards Malkin Tower. They each carried a net and a club. They were looking forward to using them.

Alice Nutter and the herbalist were already at the tower. Alice on her cob, the herbalist on her donkey. They had agreed that Alice would argue with the guards at the front of the tower while the herbalist made her way unseen to the north part at the rear, where she knew the secret way in and out.

The herbalist let her donkey go to eat new shoots on the hawthorn, and was not surprised to see Jennet Device sitting leaning against the tower. The child regarded her and said nothing. She was used to grown people wanting something from her.

'Jennet! I know you can go inside.'

'What if I can?'

'Then go inside and get the poppet your mother has made!'

The child shook her head. 'I can't do that. It is enchanted.'

'But not to you. And if you bring it I shall give you something good.'

The child looked interested. The herbalist took a chicken leg out of her pocket. She threw it to the child who caught it in one hand and devoured it, bones complete, all the while keeping her eyes on the herbalist.

'And that was only the leg. You shall eat the whole bird. And you shall have this sixpence.' She took out the big shiny coin that still bore the image of Elizabeth.

Without a word Jennet disappeared as if into the air. The herbalist sat down. She would have to wait.

✳

At the south of the tower Alice Nutter remonstrated with the guards to let her in; it was her property. The guards refused. As this row increased, the band inside the tower crowded to the slits to watch. The head and the poppet were left untended.

Jennet, wriggling like a fish, poked up from below and saw the scene. The head was on the table. The poppet was propped behind it near to the ladder entrance to the cellar.

Jennet was as fast a thief as the rest of her Demdike clan, and smaller and lighter. In a second she had the poppet and was down the steps and out through the concealed hole and up in the ditch beyond. She threw the poppet at the herbalist who pulled out the pins, and put it into her saddlebag, and urged the donkey away. Jennet got her sixpence and her chicken. She took both with her into the bushes.

At Read Hall Roger Nowell was stirring. He could move his legs. He was still in a fever but he was no longer paralysed.

✳

Tom Peeper and Constable Hargreaves rode slowly up to Malkin Tower. Neither man was pleased to see Alice Nutter.

'We're here on Crown business to take the prisoners to Read Hall,' said Constable Hargreaves in his lumbering way, 'and you may not enter the tower. If you have any argument you must address it to the Magistrate.'

'She'll be summoned there soon enough,' said Tom Peeper.

Alice turned on him. 'You have neither manners nor charm nor looks nor brains nor skill, and yet you are alive, while many women who did nothing but spin and weave and do their best have been hanged or burned. Can you explain that to me?'

'I am not a witch, Mistress,' said Tom Peeper. 'As for looks, can you explain yours to me?'

Alice struck him across the face with her riding crop. He wiped the blood away and spat at her. 'You'll be burning soon enough.'

Before Alice could reply, the guards had planked the drawbridge across the fetid moat and opened the door into the tower. Elizabeth Device was first out.

'She has certainly lost her looks,' said Peeper. 'Not that Squinting Lizzie ever had any. She should be grateful to any man that threw her a kiss the way you would throw a dog a week-old bone.'

'Alice Nutter, save me!' shouted Elizabeth Device.

'You think she'll fly you away, do you?' said Constable Hargreaves. 'Too late for flying work now.'

As Elizabeth came near, Tom Peeper coshed her on the shoulders. She fell down, cursing.

The other captives were led out. Constable Hargreaves threw his net over them to the front; Tom Peeper netted the rest to the rear. And so they were caught, like human fish, with a guard on either side. Miserable, ragged and afraid, they set off to Read Hall.

Alice watched them go. Elizabeth Device turned round, her face defeated and furious, blood running from her ear. 'Alice Nutter! Save me or be damned with me!'

The Past

The unhappy band disappeared down the slope away from the tower. Alice walked round it, looking for the herbalist, but she had gone. Alice stood by the bush that concealed Jennet Device, but the child was still as a toad. Only her watchful eyes moved.

God, it was a dreadful spot. Alice hated it. She should have pulled it down. She would have pulled it down if Old Demdike had not begged her to leave it where it stood.

And Demdike had reason – of a kind. Her grandmother and her mother had taken refuge here.

Malkin Tower was the wild and forsaken place

where Isolde de Heton had come with her baby when she was an outcast from the abbey at Whalley, a fallen woman, a Sataniser.

Here, with her fierce lover Blackburn, she had raised her child, shunned by all society. She was a noblewoman but they shunned her.

Here, days, nights, weeks, months, alone, she taught her child Bess Blackburn to scorn the crowd and to exult in loneliness. When Blackburn himself came back on his infrequent visits from raiding and robbing, the tower was lit up, and fearful passers-by claimed they saw imps circling the tower like bats. There were strange noises, laughter, shouting. And whenever Blackburn departed again, Isolde and Bess had new clothes and fresh horses and they rode about Pendle Forest and Pendle Hill away from the paths and tracks. If you saw them they would not speak to you.

Isolde died – or was spirited away, some say – by her demon lover. Her daughter Bess was sixteen then and, tiring of a solitary life, took the money piled in the tower – a substantial sum – and used it for a dowry to marry a man in Whalley.

Bess Blackburn gave birth to one child. A daughter. She christened her Elizabeth after herself, though some say that Old Demdike was christened twice, once for God and once for Satan, in the black pool at the foot of Pendle Hill.

Alice walked quickly round to the front of the tower. She entered, and stood in the awful room. The walls were black with smoke, shiny with grease, green with mildew.

She noticed a recess in the wall of the tower with a sack curtain drawn across it. Alice pulled back the curtain. It concealed a sleeping compartment, surprisingly clean and made comfortable with clean straw. The walls were drawn from top to bottom with alchemical drawings and hieroglyphs.

Alice studied the wall. She could read it. For a moment she forgot where she was and thought she was back at Bankside and she and Elizabeth were casting planetary conjunctions.

Here on the wall were moon calendars and calculations of the stars. Here was Demdike's own astrological nativity. And here underneath it was

Alice's nativity, though not her name. With a shock Alice saw that the date of her death had been numbered too.

She backed out of the recess and drew the curtain. She was sweating. She turned into the room. It was dusk. The Daylight Gate.

There was a faint green luminescence coming from the rough table. It was the head.

She could not believe what she was looking at. The empty eye sockets, the collapsed nose, the fetid boiled skin that hung in strips off the skull. The mouth hole propped open with a stick, and the fat black tongue protruding out. Robert Preston's tongue.

Alice had to hold herself upright and not vomit. There was no sound but her own short breath.

The loose mouth on the head seemed to twitch. The black tongue moved slowly up and down in the belched hole.

Then the head spoke. 'Born in fire. Warmed by fire. By fire to depart.'

Alice cried out and ran from the tower, unhitched

her pony and galloped down the slope without looking back.

The child Jennet Device poked her head up from the cellar and went up to the head. She patted it. She put the baby's hand in front of its sagging mouth and sat down with her back against the wall to finish her chicken, singing a lullaby to herself that she knew from somewhere.

Thomas Potts of
Chancery Lane

*The examination of Elizabeth Device of the Forest of Pendle
in the County of Lancaster. Widow. Taken at Read before
Roger Nowell Esquire. One of His Majesty's Justices of the
Peace in the said County.*

'The servants of Satan,' said Potts as the troop
from Malkin Tower were brought into the hall at
Read. 'I have spoken already to the one they call
Old Demdike. She sits in the gaol at Lancaster and
does not ask for mercy. This is her daughter, you
say. Then this is the one we should catch before
the others.'

Roger Nowell nodded. He had no aches or pains now. He had not believed that a man could be laid low by witchcraft until he felt it in his body. Now he believed.

Potts began his work. He accused Elizabeth Device of treason. Did she not know the Witchcraft Act of 1604?

She was silent.

Potts enlightened her. 'It is a capital offence, punishable by death, to conjure a spirit.'

Elizabeth Device said she had conjured no spirits and knew none.

'And what of Old Demdike's Familiar, Tibbs? And what of Ball, that belongs to you, they say, a small brown dog?'

There was a dog. There were plenty of dogs. She would not have it.

'And what of the making of pictures of clay?'

She had made no pictures of clay.

'And what of the maiming of John Law, Pedlar, by your daughter Alizon?'

She was not responsible for her own daughter nor for her own mother.

'Call James Device,' said Potts.

Jem came in. He had not run away on two legs or eight. He looked around at the finery of the hall. He was out of place, drunk, bewildered. But he knew what to do.

POTTS: 'Have you a Familiar that serves you?'

JEM: 'His name is Dandy. He is a dog.'

POTTS: 'What does he do for you?'

JEM: 'Fetches me things.'

ELIZABETH DEVICE: 'And that is what a dog is for, you oaf!'

POTTS: 'Silence here! James Device – do you confirm that your mother, Elizabeth Device, on Good Friday, called the Meeting at Malkin Tower?'

JEM: 'She did do.'

POTTS: 'And to what purpose?'

JEM: 'To make a plot to deliver those in prison.'

POTTS: 'Anything else?'

JEM: 'To kill the gaoler there.'

POTTS: 'Anything else?'

JEM: 'To conjure a spirit but she did not conjure a spirit.'

ELIZABETH: 'You creeping piece of soiled earth! He lies!'

POTTS: 'Why would he lie?'

ELIZABETH: 'To save himself, you London fool!'

POTTS stood up. He was short but he stood up and drew himself to his full height. 'I will not be abused by a witch and a trollop.'

ELIZABETH: 'I am glad to hear it, for I am neither the one nor the other.'

POTTS: 'Do you deny the charges against you?'

ELIZABETH: 'I deny them.'

POTTS: 'You, James Device, will you testify against your mother?'

JEM: 'I will.'

POTTS: 'And against all gathered here that were at Malkin Tower?'

JEM: 'I will.'

POTTS: 'Then there is little more to say. Magistrate! I recommend that you commit this Malkin-trash to the prison and we shall hear them again, before a Judge, at the Lancaster Assizes.'

ELIZABETH: 'If he is testifying against me, then I

am testifying against him. He escaped Malkin Tower by turning himself into a hare!'

There was silence in the room. Jem started to laugh. 'I am safe, aren't I, Constable Hargreaves, and Tom? There's nothing anyone will do to me. I'll go home now and look after Jennet.'

There was silence in the room. Hargreaves was looking at the floor. Tom Peeper was looking out of the window. Potts looked up from where he was busily writing his notes. 'Take James Device away with the rest. The Judge will decide.'

Jem bolted for the window, but it was too late. Strong hands held him. He looked imploringly, uncomprehendingly at Tom Peeper. 'You said I would get a billet at a farm, and a suit of clothes, and food, and a sweetheart . . .'

Tom Peeper laughed. 'If the Judge lets you off, maybe you will. But your own mother has admitted you changed into a hare, and, Your Honour, that is what he told me too, but I thought he was drunk.'

'Shape-shifting is common,' said Potts. 'Temporary but common. I have his own confession, now corroborated by his mother. That is sufficient.'

Elizabeth Device started laughing. A high mad laugh. 'Well done, my fine fellow out of my womb. What have you gained? Nothing! And oh, what have you lost? Everything!'

'There's Jennet!' shouted Jem. 'She has to be fed and cared for.'

Tom Peeper stepped forward. 'I will take her on, Your Honours.'

Elizabeth laughed again, harsh and sick. 'Will you then, after all these years? Well, well, and after all, you are her father.'

Roger Nowell looked aghast. Tom Peeper looked shifty. Constable Hargreaves looked at his boots. James Device had his mouth open. Then he closed his mouth, took his fists from his pockets and knocked down Tom Peeper with a single blow. The man was out cold on the floor.

'There is one good thing you have done in your stinking life,' said Elizabeth Device. 'And it was no romance, gentlemen. Tom Peeper raped me. Said I should be glad of it, looking as I do.'

Jem turned to her with hatred. 'You let me sell your own daughter to her own father.'

'You would have sold her to someone,' said Elizabeth. 'At least he bought her a dress now and then.'

Roger Nowell stood up. 'Enough. Get them out of here. The child Jennet will sleep and eat in my kitchen for the time being.' He looked down at Tom Peeper. 'Hargreaves, go and throw that live vermin into the pond. If he drowns, let him. If not, keep him out of my sight.'

Hargreaves had his men lift up the senseless body.

'You from Malkin,' said Roger Nowell, 'you will leave here at dawn except for Elizabeth Device and James Device who will leave at noon. Take them to the cellars. Feed them.'

'There is one missing,' said Elizabeth.

'There is another witch?' said Potts. 'If you testify it will go in your favour.'

'You lie!' shouted Jem.

'Will you make me a promise and have it witnessed?' said Elizabeth Device.

Potts motioned for the others to be led away. Now there were only the three of them in the room.

'I want no stocks, no chains, no hanging, no burning,' said Elizabeth. 'Write it down. Witness it, Master Nowell.'

'Who is it?' said Potts. 'Who is the witch?'

'Alice Nutter,' said Elizabeth Device.

The Hourglass Running

Alice Nutter returned to the Rough Lee. The herbalist was waiting for her with the poppet.

'Now do you believe me?'

Alice nodded. She was shaking. She did not tell her about the head. 'Will you help me?'

Together they packed the chest with silver and clothes, and had the stable boys load it onto a cart hitched to the herbalist's donkey, and away she went with money to take two horses and a coach to Manchester the next morning.

Alice secured her jewels and cash and deeds of deposit in a soft leather bag and hid the bag in the passage that connected her study and bedroom. She took several vials of liquid from her cupboard, and as she did so, she saw Edward Kelley's letter where she had put it on the day that it burned.

She took it out.

And if thou callest him, like unto an angel of the north wearing a dark costume, he will hear thee and come to thee. Yet meet him where he may be met — at the Daylight Gate.

She put the letter inside her dress.

Then she opened a small box and took out a tiny mirror. The mirror had a silver rim and a silver back and its glass was made of mercury. This was the mirror that John Dee had given her.

There was one thing left: the vial of elixir.

She went to bed. She turned her hourglass to start its running. She would rise by 2 a.m. and be gone before three o'clock.

And Running Out

It was around nine o'clock at night when Christopher Southworth rode into Lancaster.

He lodged his horse at the Red Lion near Gallows Hill, took a room for himself and ate bread and meat. Then leaving unnoticed on foot he made his way to Lancaster Castle.

It was easy enough to get past the sentries. The fog had not lifted. He was as good as invisible. He had a rope and a hook and he scaled the wall. He had done this before.

He found the Well Dungeon by the grating in the ground.

He lay down. 'Jane!'

Jane Southworth was standing in her customary spot under the grating, waiting for rain. She heard her name. Now she knew she had gone mad. The voice came again. 'Jane!'

She looked up the thirty feet to the grating. She could see nothing. Then she heard the grating being lifted away. She looked round. The others were asleep but for Nance Redfern who was somewhere with the gaoler.

A rope dropped down into the dungeon. Down the rope came Christopher Southworth.

'Jane!' He threw his arms around her. She knew then that she must be dead. 'Jane, climb onto my back and we will be gone. Hurry!'

She looked at him, shaking her head. 'Is it you, Kit? Am I dead?'

He gave her water and she drank the whole flask. He gave her a piece of meat that she ate slowly, never taking her eyes off him. He told her that she was not dead. That he had come from France to rescue her.

'It is a plot,' she said. 'They had a child accuse me of holding the Black Mass. My maid accused me of sticking pins into a poppet. They will find any way to ruin the Southworths.'

He held her to him. She was bones and filth. He wanted to cry and he wanted to tear the dungeon apart with his hands.

'Catch hold fast to my body. I have strength to pull us both out of here. We shall go at once to London and then to France.'

She shook her head. 'If I stand trial I may be acquitted. If I escape with you tonight, even if we are not caught, then they will claim it as witchcraft.'

'What of it?'

'Then they have won. If they win others will suffer. And do you believe that they do not know you are here?'

'They are looking for me in Pendle. Not here. Come with me.'

Old Demdike woke up. Her eyes were filmy with cataracts but she could see the tall dark outline of Christopher Southworth. 'It is the Dark Gentleman! I knew he would come!'

Alizon Device roused herself, rubbed her eyes

and stared at Christopher. Chattox snored on.

Old Demdike struggled to her feet numb in their rags, and shoved her stinking body up against him. 'I knew you would not abandon me!'

Christopher pushed her off. 'Get away from me, you hag! Which one are you?'

'Demdike. I am Demdike! You have my Soul. Here is my body.'

Her hair was matted. Her skin was thin and lined with red vein marks round her nose and cheeks. Hairs grew from her moles. Her neck had joined her shoulders. The rest was a shapeless mass.

He did not know what to say or what to do. Was this the lover of his lover?

She put out her hand. One finger was missing. It was the third finger of her left hand . . . '*Remember me . . .*'

He remembered the ring on Alice's finger, her skin smooth and clear.

He looked at Old Demdike again. She had green eyes. Eyes like a pool in Pendle Forest. Eyes like the forest when it rains and the sky is green and the earth is green and the air is green. She had green eyes.

Jane would not go with him. She asked him for a Bible and he gave her his missal. He gave her money to bribe the gaoler for food and water. He took off his cloak and wrapped it round her.

There were noises outside. He had to leave. He kissed Jane and climbed rapidly up the rope hand over hand. He was strong and agile. He hauled himself out at the top and lay on the stones level with the grating. He could hear them below.

'It was the Dark Gentleman!'

'Then why didn't he take us?'

'He will, I tell you he will!'

He lay on the stones, his heart beating. Life was an intervention. At every moment the chances change. If Jane were with him now. If they were escaping together. If James had not come to the throne. If the Gunpowder Plot had never happened. If Elizabeth had not executed Mary. If Henry had not wanted a divorce. If the Pope had not excommunicated England. If England were a Catholic country still.

All the history, all the facts, what were they but chances? And for himself, so far, he was not dead. And there was Alice, who had chosen for him. If he had not come back, she would not have chosen for him.

He lay on the stones. He could change his name, his country, his faith. The tortures had changed his body. He had tried to change history.

He could not change the fact of his birth or, by very much, the fact of his death. This was his time.

He had an image of an hourglass.

Dead Time

Alice Nutter was up early. She had dressed and was ready to leave when she saw them from the window. She was in no doubt. They had come for her.

She left her precious things in their secret place and went downstairs to open the door herself. She would not hide like a coward. Let them come for her. She would leave of her own free will. She would not be taken.

At Read Hall Roger Nowell had blazed up the fire. The room was warm and bright. He bowed. She curtsied. He asked her to sit down. Potts came in, his eyes like spears. He asked her if she had read the King's book *Daemonology*.

Alice replied that she had. She added that she had no great opinion of it.

'Then I will ask you to pay attention as follows,' said Potts, reading from his own copy.

'*The two degrees of persons which chiefly practise Witch-craft are such: as are in great miserie or poverty, for such the Devil allures to follow him, by promising great riches, and worldly commoditie: Others, though riche, yet burne in a desperate desire of Power or Revenge. But to attempt a woman in this sort, the Devil had small means . . . How she was drawn to fall to this wicked course, I know not, but she is now come to receive her trial for her vile and damnable practices.*'

'There is no evidence against me,' said Alice.

Roger Nowell lifted his hand and Constable Hargreaves brought in James and Elizabeth Device. Neither had slept.

They were asked to identify Alice as coming to Malkin Tower on Good Friday. They were asked to say her business there, and Elizabeth agreed that Alice Nutter had always been a friend to her mother, Old Demdike.

'She is more powerful even than her!' shouted Jem.

'I am not a witch,' said Alice. 'I have nothing else to say.'

'What do you say to this?' said Roger Nowell.

Constable Hargreaves brought in the poppet. Elizabeth Device looked pale. 'I didn't make no poppet,' she shouted.

'It is a crude likeness to myself,' said Roger Nowell. 'And yesterday I was struck with disease and agony.'

'Bring in the herbalist from Whalley,' said Potts.

Alice's friend came into the hall. Roger Nowell had her stand before him. 'Did you not say yesterday that my ague was no ordinary illness but witchcraft?'

The herbalist nodded. She did not look at Alice.

'Then what do you say of this doll found at Mistress Nutter's house? Her servant brought it here.'

Potts took the doll and examined it. 'This is witchcraft. Alice Nutter, did you fashion this doll?'

'I did not.'

'Then how is it that it came to be in the study of your house?'

Alice could not answer; she could not incriminate her friend the herbalist.

'The doll has a scalp of human hair. I do not know how you robbed the graves,' said Potts.

James Device shouted out: 'I robbed them! She bewitched me to the form of a hare and I escaped Malkin Tower, and robbed the graves at Newchurch in Pendle and brought her teeth and the rest. She bewitched me. Let me go free like the spider said.'

'The spider?' asked Potts. 'Is that your Familiar?'

'You all said if I testified against Alice Nutter I should go free.'

'So that is it,' said Alice. 'Bribery and intimidation – but all legal because the Law is doing it.'

Potts stood up. 'Alice Nutter. You are accused of witchcraft. You will stand trial at the Lancaster Assizes.'

Roger Nowell stood up. 'Clear the room.'

Alice Nutter sat still. They left one by one, and Potts too, until only Alice and Roger Nowell remained. It was not yet five o'clock in the morning.

'So you have me,' said Alice. 'I do not know why.'

Roger Nowell smiled. 'I have you, but I could let you go.'

'What is the price of my freedom?'

'Christopher Southworth.'

'He is not at my house. You searched it.'

'But you know where he is, don't you?'

'I do not know where he is.'

'Your groom tells me you lent him a horse yesterday.'

'Jem Device says I turned him into a hare. Do you believe that too?'

Roger Nowell was silent for a moment. Then he said, 'Sir John Southworth is my friend. I take no pleasure in this. My own situation is threatened. Do you not see that? Christopher Southworth came to Lancashire and he came to you. You imagine I do not have my spies? You hid him six years ago when he fled London after the Plot – yes, I know you did so, and it is true I turned a blind eye. They caught him when he left you for the coast of Wales. He would not confess who it was who had hidden him. He did not give your name.'

Alice felt the tears in her eyes as she thought of his tortured body. Roger Nowell noticed them and he came towards her.

'It does not surprise me that he loves you.' He put his arms out to her. She neither yielded nor resisted. He said softly, 'You think your servants cannot be bought like every other servant?'

Alice looked at him. 'Did you have Jane Southworth arrested?'

Roger Nowell shook his head. 'Potts.' There was a pause. 'I had reason to believe that Christopher Southworth was returning to Lancashire. I did not know why. Frankly, I thought he had gone mad. Then Potts came with his witchery popery popery witchery. I am caught in this trap every bit as much as you are. There has to be a sacrifice – don't you understand that?'

And in her mind she was in the house at Vauxhall and Elizabeth was saying, 'She is the One.'

Still Alice did not speak. Roger Nowell stood back, took a bag from his pocket, and drew out the heavy silver crucifix. He swung it from side to side like a pendulum; like an omen of time. 'This was found in your bed.'

'A witch with a crucifix. Am I accused of the Black Mass or the High Mass?'

Roger Nowell kissed her forehead. He felt her body resist him. 'Potts makes no distinction and neither does our Scottish King. Whatever you are, you are facing death.'

'I am not afraid.'

Roger Nowell drew back from her. 'I am going to give you a chance. Go home. Think carefully. Run away and I will hunt you down. Return at dusk and tell me where to look for Christopher Southworth – that is all – and you will be in your own bed tonight. Refuse, and I will send you to Lancaster Castle.'

Bankside

Christopher Southworth had arrived in London. He came through the turnpike at Highgate, sold his horse and walked down into the city.

Stables, kennels, breweries, carpenters' shops, pudding dens, low-roofed sheds where they sewed jerkins or rolled candles. Inns, taverns, bakers, cook shops, men and women smoking clay pipes carrying fish baskets on their heads. Dogs running in and out of the cartwheels, a parrot on a perch, a woman selling bolts of cloth from a cart. A tinker with pots and pans hung round his thin body. A fiddler playing a melody. A sheep on a rope, the smell of mutton flesh cooking, the smell of iron being heated till it glowed. A little boy with bare feet, a girl carrying a baby, two soldiers, ragged and thin.

Soon he reached the River Thames, wide like a dream, jammed with boat-craft and bodies, like a nightmare.

There was a boatyard at Bankside. Boats upended, sanded, oiled, the smell of pitch heating in a vast pot. At the boatyard two men in dresses were joking with a charcoal burner who wanted to go and see a play.

Christopher Southworth went up to them and asked where was the House at the Sign. 'What's it to you?' said one, and he gave them a penny, and they pointed to a stumpy pier where a cowhand was branding his cow in a hiss of steam.

The house was timber. Pitch-painted frame, in-filled with plaster, with handsome glass and lead windows. A woman was leaving the house. He introduced himself, showed her Alice's seal and letter and key, and although she seemed surprised, she let him in. He told her his name was Peter Northless.

'If it is True North you are looking for, you have come to the right place,' she said, reaching down and feeling for his balls. His hand stopped her. She laughed. 'We shall not disturb you unless you wish to be disturbed.'

He went in. He understood. This was a brothel.

And a handsome brothel. Well appointed. There was a staircase up to a gallery with neat doors leading off it. So this was how Alice kept up her income. She said she got a good rent for the place.

He went up to the gallery. This was not the floor she had described. A room at the top, Alice had said.

He came to a little swing door. He pushed through it and found a flight of stairs, narrow and unused, if dust was a guide. His footsteps left prints on the treads.

He went up, and up, impossibly up, it seemed, and at the top of the stairs he was faced with a big sturdy square door entirely painted with a face. The keyhole was in the right eye of the face. He looked at the face. The face looked at him.

Christopher went in.

There was a high bed against a square-panelled wall. A table by the window set for two people but thick with dust. A portrait of a beautiful woman with green eyes. 'Elizabeth Southern,' he said, amazed that this was the hag he had pushed away in Lancaster Gaol.

He felt he was intruding on another life. A secret life.

There was a calfskin book on the table. He opened it. It was Alice's handwriting.

John Dee has returned to Poland to rejoin Edward Kelley. There is no news of Elizabeth. I have succeeded in making the mirror.

The mirror?

He looked around. There was a mirror on the wall, but nothing unusual about it. There were no cupboards in this room. No drawers in the table. Perhaps she had taken the mirror with her. Perhaps it had been stolen or lost.

Well, she would be here tomorrow or the next day, and on the day after, they would ride to Dover and sail to Calais.

The room had long windows to the side that opened onto a rough square balcony. He freed them from years of neglect and went outside. He could see the river winding through the city, and all the teeming life of London rolled out like a carpet. He felt peaceful and suddenly very tired. He had ridden hard, changing horses, hardly sleeping. Now he could sleep. After all, it was Alice's bed.

The Daylight Gate

Stand on the flat top of Pendle Hill and you can see everything of the county of Lancashire. Some say you can see other things too. This is a haunted place. The living and the dead come together on the hill.

Alice knew she was being followed. Let them follow her. They would not come too near.

She heard wings. She held out her arm. It was her bird. He scarred her arm where she had no glove but she did not care because she loved him and she knew that love leaves a wound that leaves a scar.

She had the letter from Edward Kelley. *Yet meet him*

where he may be met — at the Daylight Gate.

'I have come,' she said.

For a while nothing happened. The mist that wraps the hill close like a cloak was up to the belly of her pony. She dismounted and stood holding the reins. There was no sound. It was as if the hill was listening.

Then she saw a shape coming towards her. Hooded. Swift. Her heart was beating hard. The falcon flew up into a blasted tree.

The figure stopped a few feet away from Alice and threw back its hood. It was John Dee.

'I did not expect to see you,' said Alice.

'Who were you expecting?'

'I have a letter . . . from Edward . . .'

'One of his summoning spirits, I expect,' said John Dee. 'None such can help you now.'

'Are you alive?' said Alice.

John Dee shook his head. 'Not as you are. We are standing on a strip of time, what the Catholics call Limbo — in between the worlds of the living and the dead.'

'Am I dead then?' said Alice.

'I am here to set you free. Your body is a shell. Leave it behind. Give me your hand. Let them find your shell abandoned on the ground. They can do nothing to your body once you have deprived them of your Soul.'

'I never believed in the Soul,' said Alice.

'Still stubborn,' said John Dee.

'Where is Christopher? Is he safe?'

'He is in your house at Bankside.'

Alice Nutter smiled. Then he was safe. He would set sail. 'And Elizabeth?'

'It is too late for Elizabeth. It was too late long ago.'

'Release her from that rotting place.'

'I cannot. Nor can you. There is nothing you can do now, Alice. It is time to go.'

John Dee held out his hand.

She stood in the mist and the failing light. There were only two people she cared about. Christopher was safe. She would never see him again, she knew. Elizabeth was left behind.

She whistled. Her falcon came reluctantly and

landed with her on that thin strip of time. She took the gold ring from her finger and fastened it to the bird's foot. 'Find him,' she said. 'Tell him I cannot come.'

Out of the mist she could hear voices. They were near. John Dee held out his hand like a fiery branch. All she had to do was touch the fire and the prophecy would be ended. She would not burn at the stake. She would be free.

She shook her head. She put her foot into the stirrup and swung up onto her pony. She would not let Elizabeth go.

Love is as strong as death.

The Knocking at the Gate

She was dressed in magenta. She rode side-saddle on her copper mare. She brought a small bag. She rode through the arch into the courtyard at Read Hall scattering the servants around her.

It was night. She was late.

The men in the house heard the sound of a horse. They heard knocking at the door. A servant opened the door. They heard his cries of alarm. Roger Nowell got up to see what was the commotion. He opened the door from his small study onto the wide hall.

Alice Nutter had ridden straight in. The mare stood among the benches of the hall, pawing the stone, her ears forward and haughty.

Potts came out. Potts went back in again.

Alice Nutter dismounted and gave the reins of her horse to Roger Nowell. 'I am ready,' she said.

And a Bird

When Christopher Southworth awoke there was a girl in his bed. Not exactly in his bed; she was lying on his pillows like a pet dog.

'I've always wanted to get into this room. It's haunted, you know. All the girls know it's haunted.'

'Who haunts it?'

'Two dead people. Two women. You hear them laughing and moving about up here. In the evening. And you hear the bed creak. They was sold to the Devil.'

'I know the women,' said Christopher. 'They are not dead.'

'Well then, how are they here every full-moon night?'

'It is full moon tonight. I shall be here. Ask me tomorrow.'

The girl nodded and got up. 'You want sex or anything? No charge. As you are a special guest.'

He shook his head. 'I am in love with someone.'

'That's a pretty reply. I hope someone says that of myself some day.'

As she was going he called her back. 'Why do they call this place the House at the Sign?'

'It's not the sign of the cross if that's what you was thinking — we're not religious here.' She laughed. 'On the front step you'll see it. The pentagram. Alchemical something.'

She was gone.

He went about London that day. He engaged the horses to take himself and Alice down to Dover to where his passage to Calais waited at anchor. He felt hopeful. He did not know why.

When he got back to the House at the Sign, he looked down, and sure enough, on the great wide flagstone at the front door, there was a pentagram with a face inside it, like the face on the door. And there were runes he couldn't read. Alice would tell him when she arrived. He hoped she would come today.

A few of the girls were about, but the place was quiet. He liked it here, set back in its pretty garden, with the river flowing along. She liked to live near water, did Alice. And a witch cannot endure water, he thought, and then he asked himself, 'Do I believe in witches?' He did not like that question. The question that followed he liked less: If Alice is a witch, how can I love her? He would love her if she were a wolf that tore out his heart. And he wondered what that said about love.

He reached the topmost stair and the door with the face regarded him. He smiled and ran his finger playfully over the mouth. The mouth was not made of wood; it was soft.

He recoiled, crying out, holding his hand. Soft?

Forcing himself to do it, he touched the mouth of the door again; it was good solid wood.

He went inside, leaving the door open, poured water into the bowl and washed his face. As he turned to look back at the door, it closed.

He refused to be afraid but he *was* afraid. He

went over to the windows that opened onto the square balcony. Perched on the wooden rail was the falcon.

Christopher was delighted. He felt his body untense. Alice was near. She would never leave without her bird.

He got water. He gave it a piece of pork he had bought. The bird ate and drank. Christopher was talking to it about France, and the hawks it would meet there. Everything would be different, changed.

Then the bird lifted its foot and Christopher saw the ring. '*Remember me.*'

With great care he cut the ring away and held it in his hand. The bird regarded him. Alice would never have parted with this ring unless she had no other way of telling him.

'They have taken her . . .' he said.

Torture Me

They had her naked, on her feet, her hands strapped above her head, her back towards them. They wore hoods. They carried long sharp awls.

'Follow the points on either side of the spine.'

The first man rammed the metal spike of the awl into Alice's back. He twisted it out. He stood back, pleased with his demonstration. 'That's how you do it. Now you.'

His apprentice was hesitant. He was only a boy. He pushed his awl clumsily into the other side of Alice's spine. Blood flowed.

'Be firmer, boy! Try again and stab it straight down the back, one after another, an inch apart. You want to shove it right into the skin and flesh and muscle — that's it, good and deep. Leave the buttocks. We'll flay those.'

They bled her until her back was a mass of raised welts and running blood. She could taste blood in her mouth where she had bitten her tongue to stop herself crying out.

She heard a door open behind her — she couldn't turn round because her hands and feet were tied. She heard a light pleasant voice she did not recognise. 'Where is Christopher Southworth?' Alice did not answer. The voice said, 'I would like to show you a skinning.'

She was untied and blindfolded. Naked, barefoot, she was led through the lower dungeons where they kept the racks and the thumbscrews. They took off her blindfold. The iron maiden was open in front of her; an upright coffin, its inner front lid studded with six-inch iron nails. 'Nothing to worry about,' said the voice. 'Mainly for display.'

They walked her on. 'We could break every bone in your body one by one. We could pull out your teeth one by one. We could tear off your fingernails — one by one. We could slowly lower you piece by piece into boiling oil. We can ram you with a poker – sometimes heated, sometimes spiked. But that sounds unkind, doesn't it? We would prefer to treat you well.'

She heard a squealing. 'The rat room,' he said.

She looked through the grille into the room, if room it was. It was piled with rats about three feet deep, eating each other. 'Poor things, they have nothing else to eat but each other. I would not dream of throwing you in such a place. Not all of you at once. Look, we have slots here where we can push through an arm or a leg. One limb at a time.'

Alice did not speak. A light gentle hand stroked her agonised back. She winced. The hand stopped at the top of her buttocks. 'We're not going to rape you.'

They passed on. Alice could hear breathing, rapid and laboured. A hand pulled back a curtain.

A man lay tied down to a bench. He was clothed but for his left leg. His eyes were wild and bloodshot. His lips were flecked with foam. He turned his head, saw and did not see Alice.

His persecutor was bending over him absorbed in his work. He had already removed the skin from the man's upper thigh and was intent on pulling it carefully over his knee. Alice could see the large thigh muscle pulsing with pain. The torturer made a quick incision. The man cried out and fainted as the torturer pulled the stocking of skin down the lower leg towards the foot.

'Finish that leg, leave the other till tomorrow,' said the voice. 'Oh, and wake him up.'

A boy stepped forward with a bucket of water and flung it in the man's unconscious face. He opened his eyes.

Alice was led away to a furnished room. She was given wine. She refused it. She was told to bend over. She saw a sturdy pair of legs, feet planted apart. Her arms were pulled over her head and held tightly. She heard a swish. The man with the pleasant voice began to thrash her buttocks. 'All we want to know is where he is.'

When she came to she was back in her cell lying face down. She did not know whether it was day or night, or how many days or nights had passed. There was water and food put out for her. She drank but did not eat.

Shadows

It was late. Christopher Southworth was watching the moon rise. The bird was with him. He wanted to send something to Alice to tell her that he would come. 'You will go to her, won't you?' he said to the bird that sat perched and silent.

As the full moon shone into the chamber behind him, he heard laughter. He looked round and into the room. There was Alice seated at the table with Elizabeth Southern. They were about to carve a chicken. His heart leapt. He ran through the door. There was no one there.

He stood looking around, passed his hand over his face, took a drink. He went back outside.

The moment he was out of the room again he

heard music. He looked back; Alice and Elizabeth were dancing together. This time he did not rush in, he watched them. The room was exactly as he knew it, but there were flowers, and everything seemed pretty and vital, not dusty and abandoned. Alice kissed Elizabeth. He felt himself dizzy with jealousy. They moved towards the bed. Alice touched Elizabeth's neck.

He could not contain himself. He jumped into the room. It was empty.

He sat on the bed, his head in his hands.

It was then that he heard a step on the stair. 'Let me in, quick!'

He recognised the girl's voice. He opened the door. She slipped inside. 'I come to warn you. There's half a dozen men downstairs asking questions. I'd get gone if I was you. I'll pretty them up, kiss them and the like. That'll give you a few minutes.'

He nodded and squeezed her hand. She left. He put on his boots and jacket and slung his flasks of water and wine either side of his body. He stuffed the cheese and bread he had bought into his bag and put out the candle on the table. The moon was bright enough to light up everything.

He looked out of the front window of the room. Yes. There were men in the yard in front of the house talking to some of the women.

He went out onto the disused balcony. He could climb up on the roof. He fished in his pocket and took out a French coin. He held it in the palm of his hand and the bird took it. 'Tell her I will come,' he said.

Understanding him, the falcon flew up to the roof and, finding its north, opened its powerful wings and was gone.

No More

Old Demdike was dying. She had a fever. She had seen no sunlight for three months. She had lived on dirty water, foul bread and bloated rats.

The gaoler who brought Alice her food and drink told her about Demdike. 'I would like to see her,' said Alice. 'I will pay.'

That night the gaoler came with his dripping flare and led Alice from her upper cell to the Well Dungeon. He said nothing. He opened the door. He fixed the flare lit with pig-fat to the iron ring in the wall. Then he locked Alice in.

At first she could not see. Then she became

aware of a heap of bodies, continuous, undistin-guishable, lying in heaps for warmth. Chattox, Nance Redfern, Jem Device, Elizabeth Device. Names that meant nothing. The occupants of those names had vacated them.

She leaned against the wall to steady herself against the stench and the filth. As her eyes got used to the malicious dark, she saw a woman standing quite still under light so little it was like a memory of light.

Alice made her way over the motionless bodies. The statue-woman was Jane Southworth. She was holding a prayer book so saturated with damp that it was more of a block than a book. She did not recognise Alice. Her eyes were empty. Alice put her hand on her thin shoulder but Jane brushed it away and turned back to her work of looking up towards the light.

Coughing. Alice heard coughing, not a chest cough but a cough from so deep in the lungs it took the whole body with it. Demdike stirred from the mound of bodies, wrenched her guts and spat. She pulled herself up onto her knees.

Alice went to her. The smell was overpowering. 'Elizabeth,' she said. 'Elizabeth.'

Old Demdike looked up. She was almost blind but she could hear. 'He's coming for me, Alice,' she said. 'Has he sent you?'

'No one is coming for you,' said Alice. 'Drink this.'

She had brought a vial of liquid. Old Demdike stuck out her tongue like a baby. Alice poured the liquid into her mouth. Demdike swallowed and shook her head. 'You can't save me now, Alice, too late.'

Yet the potion had revived her. Alice drew her to the door of the cell and put down a sack the gaoler had given her. It covered the filth. She held the wasted sick body in her arms.

'Do you remember?' said Elizabeth.

Alice remembered. About half a year after the night at the house in Vauxhall, she had heard that Elizabeth had the pox. She was with the lepers in the ruins of the old priory outside the city walls, at Bishopsgate.

It was a desolate place. A few figures roamed about, talking aloud, raving at the sky. Most were sitting or lying around low fires, too sick to move. Piles of bones and offal surrounded the separate encampments and around those piles dogs and cats and rats scavenged, only kept off by the smoky fires. When a man was too far gone in disease to light a fire the rats gnawed him where he lay.

Alice had passed further in, to where there were makeshift coverings and shacks. This was a den of lepers and drunkards, pox-ridden hags drinking a filthy mixture of beer and bad water, and raddled bucks swilling their wounds with mercury to cure their infections.

Alice found Elizabeth. She tried to give her money. Elizabeth spat at her. Alice had dropped a purse of gold at her feet but as she turned to go Elizabeth had called out, 'Alice – give me the neckcloth you are wearing.'

Now, here, in the stinking cell, Demdike started to cough and Alice loosed the rags at her neck but Demdike pulled away. 'I'll die with that at my throat closer than the noose.' In the fatty light Alice peered at the unrecognisable cloth. Demdike said, 'You gave it to me that day.'

Yes. The day in the leper house in Bishopsgate.

She was aware of something at the door.

In the room, making itself out of nothing piece by piece by piece formed a human shape. Feet, groin, chest, neck, head. The figure was dressed in grey. He wore no hat. He was short, handsome, deadly. Alice had seen him before. He gave a short bow. 'Mistress Nutter.'

Old Demdike had hidden her face. 'He has come for my Soul.'

The man opened his hand. His palm was covered in dark hair. He was holding a small clear glass bottle of blood. 'I have here the seal of our contract,' he said.

Alice tried to think. She was half mad with the torture. Everyone in this cell was wholly mad, driven out of their wits by poverty and cruelty. This was an hallucination.

The man smiled as if he knew what she was thinking. He unstoppered his little bottle and poured the blood over Demdike's head. A drop fell on Alice's hand. She felt it burning.

As the blood ran down Demdike's forehead and cheeks, she began to change. Her hair grew thick and black. Her grimy crusted eyes cleared and opened. Her skin softened and tightened. She stood up. She was Elizabeth Southern. She smiled at Alice and her eyes were green as the emeralds Alice used to wear. 'Come with me,' she said. 'We can go together. It is not far.'

The dungeon was lit up with a faint green light. The Dark Gentleman made a small bow. 'Another chance for you, Alice Nutter. Hold out your hand and it is done.'

Hardly knowing what she did, Alice held out her hand to Elizabeth. Elizabeth took it gently, but then her grip tightened like a chain. Her expression was hard and wild. 'You shall not leave me this time.'

The cell was on fire. Sheets of flame seared the walls. Fire was under her feet. The Dark Gentleman took Elizabeth's free hand and began to dance. In burning flames he and Elizabeth danced, while

Alice tried to free herself from the terrible grip. 'You shall not take her!' shouted Alice. 'I am the sacrifice and I am not dead yet.'

Alice freed both her hands and she put them either side of Elizabeth's face. She said, 'He shall not have your Soul.'

The dark man sprung at her, growling and snarling. He was like a black fox, his jaws ripping her. He was on her back, sinking his teeth into her neck. Still she held Elizabeth's face. 'Her Soul belongs to me,' she said. 'I will pay the price.'

The fiery room went black. Alice was leaning against the wall. She heard the door of the dungeon being pulled open. The gaoler entered with his flare. His face was terrified. He looked down and kicked the senseless body of Old Demdike with his foot.

There was no Elizabeth Southern. Old Demdike was dead.

Jennet Device

It had grown dark in Malkin Tower as she sat on her own, wolfing the chicken and singing a lullaby. The head and the hand were her only company. The head said, 'Jennet Device! They have all been taken to prison. Do you want them to return?' Jennet shook her own head. 'Make sure they do not,' said the head.

She went and curled up in the clean bed that belonged to Old Demdike. She had never been allowed in here. Not even her mother had been allowed in here. She was safe behind the curtain when she heard Tom Peeper opening the door of the tower, calling for her. She kept quiet. She didn't want the hard thing tonight. She was sore.

She heard him walking about. Then his footsteps stopped their pacing and he saw the head. She heard him swear. He was unsteady on his feet. He went towards the opening into the cellar. It was dark. He would fall in. She giggled. He stopped pacing. He was listening. 'Jennet?'

He found her. He pulled back the curtain to her safe place. Picked her up in his damp arms. 'Daddy fell in the pond but Daddy came back for his little girl. I've got a big bag of bread and cheese and apples and tarts from Roger Nowell's kitchen, and we'll live here safe and sound, just the two of us, Daddy and his little girl. Here, here.' He was undoing his breeches. She didn't want it in her mouth.

She slipped away from him and he came after her. The room was dark. She dodged sideways, and as he lunged to catch her, he fell through the open trapdoor into the cellar. She knew he had hurt himself.

Using all her small strength she pushed away the ladder off its mooring and down into the hole. Then she rolled her whole body under the trapdoor to move it, kneeling up with it, until by her greatest effort it reached the tipping point and banged down with a crash, sealing the cellar. There was a bolt. She shot it across the trapdoor into its keep. Then one leg by one leg she moved the rough heavy table over the trapdoor.

'Good, Jennet,' said the head. 'Now go to sleep.'

Jennet nodded, took the little hand from in front of the head and went back to her bed. All night Tom Peeper shouted, and all the next day, and the days after that, and for quite a long time, she thought, as she ate her way through a week's supply of food for two.

And then he didn't shout any more.

August 1612

'*The countie of Lancaster may lawfully be said to abound as much in witches of divers kindes, as Seminaries, Jesuits and Papists.*'

Potts was pleased with himself; he was writing a book.

'Shakespeare,' he thought as he scribbled away. 'Foolish fancy. This is life as it is lived.'

'Do you have to write a book?' asked Roger Nowell, who was sick of it all.

'Posterity. Truth. Record. Record. Truth –'

'Posterity,' said Roger Nowell.

'Here is the title page: "*The Wonderfull Discoverie of Witches in the Countie of Lancashire* by Thomas Potts, Lawyer".'

'I suppose it will take your mind off the fact that the King's spies have failed to catch Christopher Southworth – again.'

Alice Nutter was in her cell when she heard that Jane Southworth had been acquitted. Her maid had confessed that she had been put up to the accusation by a Catholic priest. As Jane Southworth was the only member of her family who was a Protestant, the accusations against her were deemed to be part of a vile papist plot. The Judge commiserated with her and ordered that she be taken home at once.

The vilest witches of the earth are the priests that consecrate crosses and ashes, water and salt, oil and cream, boughs and bones, stocks and stones; that christen bells that hang in the steeple; that conjure worms that creep in the field,' said the Judge.

Alice waited at her window all day until she saw Jane being led out to her carriage. She could barely walk.

'Jane!' shouted Alice through the bars of the window. Jane looked up. She could barely see after five months of darkness, disease and malnutrition.

'He is safe,' shouted Alice.

Jane stood for a moment, statue-like and motionless, then very slowly she raised her hand.

That evening Alice Nutter had a visitor: Roger Nowell.

'You are changed,' he said.

She had not used the elixir. She had not looked in a mirror. Now she took out the tiny mirror from her pocket and stood in the light.

Was that her? Gaunt. Lined. White hair. She was still beautiful, as if there was something transparent about her, as if her skin were made of leaves that had lain in the sun.

She was an old woman.

The Trial

When the prisoners are led into the Lancaster Assizes, Master Potts produces his prize witness: little Jennet Device.

So small and underfed is she that she has to be stood on a table to give her evidence.

One by one as they are brought in, she points them all out, the members of the coven gathered that Good Friday at Malkin Tower.

Jem Device can't walk. He hasn't walked more than twelve paces each way for four months. He has lost what fat he had. His eyes shine like fireflies in the waste ground of his body.

Chattox is demented. She spits and raves.

She curses. She wants to be what they say she is; a witch. What else is left for her to be?

Elizabeth Device believes that Satan has taken her mother. She sits in the courtroom with her hands tied, livid and vile. She still has the energy to shout obscenities.

Nance Redfern and Alizon Device lie down. They can no longer stand. Both have been infected with syphilis by the gaoler.

Mouldheels sits on the floor and pulls blisters from her pus-soaked feet. She can feel her way through to the bone.

The Bulcocks never knew if they were brother and sister or man and wife. No one told them you couldn't be both. He has his arm round her. She pulls her few strands of matted hair and hides her head. He shields what is left of her mind against what is left of his body.

Jennet Device tells the court all about their Familiars, Fancy and Dandy and Ball. She says she has flown on a broomstick and seen the Dark Gentleman with her grand-dam, Old Demdike. Jennet pays special attention to her mother. She tells the court all about the poppet and the head.

Her mother is so overcome with rage that she has to be led out of the courtroom and drenched with water. Jennet Device shows no emotion; she has no emotion to show.

Jennet looks at them. Her brother who sold her. Her mother who neglected her. Her sisters who ignored her. Chattox who frightened her. Mouldheels who stank.

She names them one by one and condemns them one by one.

Then they lead in Alice Nutter.

'Do you recognise this woman?' asks Justice Bromley. Jennet smiles and goes and takes Alice's hand. 'She has a falcon who is a spirit. She has a pony who can jump over the moon. She has food and drink and money and jewels. She is the most powerful of them all.'

Justice Bromley asks Alice Nutter how she pleads. Alice answers, 'Not guilty.' After that she remains silent.

☆

They were all convicted. Potts wrote it down. Convicted of *'practices, meetings, consultations, murthers, Charmes and villanies'*.

The End

That morning Alice Nutter was up before dawn. She had slept for an hour or so because she wanted to remember what it is like to fall asleep. What it is like to wake up.

She wanted to remember the stretch of her body. The feeling of hunger. How it felt to breathe. She was leaving home. Her body was home. She wanted to say goodbye before they evicted her.

Roger Nowell came to her cell. He said, 'Even now, if you would help us catch Christopher Southworth, I could –'

'I could not,' said Alice.

Roger Nowell looked at the floor. 'Would you like to take Communion before you are executed?'

'It is unnecessary.'

'Is there anything I can do for you?'

'I should like my magenta dress.'

The dress was brought. She wiped her face and hair with the last drops of the elixir and smashed the bottle. She dressed. She took the tiny mirror she had made out of mercury and fastened it to Christopher Southworth's crucifix. She hung the crucifix around her neck and under her dress.

She was ready.

The journey from Lancaster Gaol to the gallows east of the city was crowded. The mob were pelting and jeering, leering, mocking, and afraid too. Children were held high on their fathers' shoulders. Old women in white, to show their virtue, sat at the front of the pulsing hordes, holding up lavender and hyssop.

There were boys with buckets of cat parts; paws, tails, ears, heads, entrails. The boys went up and down the lines letting people dip in and lift out some bloody and stinking offering to hurl at the cart.

Cow dung and blood, urine, vomit and human faeces were thrown from the upper windows of those buildings that lined the route.

And all the time people were clapping and singing. This was pleasure. This was a holiday.

At the Golden Lion there were jugs of beer. The Demdike had no relatives or friends to buy for them, because everyone they knew was being executed with them, except for Jennet Device. Someone had paid for their drink though, and Alice's too. Wiping some of the filth away from their hands and faces, they drank.

Alice did not drink. She was looking out of the window. She could see a bird high in the cold morning. A steady circle of wings. It was her falcon.

The gallows were well made. The ropes were new. The drop was long. It would be quick. And then the bodies would be burned.

The first five of the women, and James Device, were led forward. Chattox and Elizabeth Device yelled curses at the mob who were pleased to see the show they had come for. James Device looked dazed and disbelieving. He was talking about a farm where he lived and where he was warm and dry and fed and soon to be married.

Alice watched the condemned as they were rough-handled onto the platform. The women struggled. Chattox was old and easy to subdue. Elizabeth Device had to be hit. The guard punched her in the face – blood ran from the cut above her eye. She was half unconscious. She was lucky. They were lined up.

Then it was quick.

Noose. Neck. Drop.

There was a roar from the crowd. James Device, tall and lanky, hadn't been fully strangled by the drop. A man's hand reached up from the front of the crowd and pulled Jem's legs. Alice heard his neck snap.

Now it was her turn. She mounted the scaffold. She did not struggle. She asked that her hands be untied and this was granted.

The hangman was fitting the others one by one and each by each into the nooses. The clergyman was asking them if they repented of the grievous sin of witchcraft.

Alice heard John Dee's voice in her head. '*Choose your death or your death will choose you.*'

It was not too late.

She lifted up her arm. The crowd beneath shouted out in fear. Was the witch cursing them? The men and women directly under the scaffold, jostling for the best view, turned and stumbled over those behind. Now there was a riot below. A man punched his neighbour and ran. A woman was trampled to death on the ground. The man who had pulled James Device by the legs and ended his misery was fighting to climb the scaffold.

Alice held up her arm, and from the sky faint with sun fell the falcon.

The bird dropped through the air, wheeled, swooped, landed straight on Alice's arm. The crowd was screaming. No one dared approach her.

Alice stared into the crowd for a second. Her hair was white. She was much changed. But in the crowd there was a face she recognised who recognised her. She smiled her old smile. She looked young again.

She stretched back her neck, exposing the long line of her throat. The falcon flapped his wings to keep himself steady as he dug his feet into her collarbone to make a perch. His head dived forward in one swift movement. He severed her jugular vein.

In the chaos of what came next, the man jumped onto the scaffold and bent over Alice's body, pulling away her dress. He lifted her head. She was wearing his crucifix. He took it off and swung it at the terrified crowd. 'Here's your witch – with a cross around her neck.'

'Catch him!' shouted Roger Nowell.

But in a bound Christopher Southworth was gone. In the terror of the crowd he could not be caught. His horse was waiting. He rode in one stretch from Lancaster to Pendle Forest. Then he tied his exhausted horse to eat and drink by the river and he climbed to the flat top of the hill. It was nearly not quite dark: the Daylight Gate.

*

He took the crucifix out of his pocket to hang it round his neck again, and it was then that he noticed the little leather case. He opened it; there was the tiny mirror made of mercury.

It was misty here. Cold now. He shivered. His breath clouded the mirror, then, as if by itself, the surface cleared. 'Alice?' he said, half fearful, half hopeful. He saw her face in the mirror.

He turned wildly. There was no one behind him.

The cold was intense, jagged. He felt like he was being cut.

They would come for him today, tomorrow or the next day.

He can hear voices. Men approaching. They are bringing nets and clubs to hunt him down like an animal. He crouches and crawls through the solid low mist where they cannot see him. His dark hair is white and dripping with mist. He is already a ghost.

Already, he knows, they will have burned her body. Already she is gone.

He squats and takes out his knife, folding back his cuffs from his wrists. Red against the white. If there is another life he will find her there.